"You're mine now."

"Yours?" Faith said incredulously. "Yours? I don't belong to anybody, Cole Cameron. You'd better get that straight."

He strode back toward her, caught her by the shoulders and took her mouth with his. She felt the power of his kiss, the heat of it...and hated herself for the soft moan she couldn't prevent.

"You're mine," he said roughly. "Sooner or later you'll admit it. And when you do, I'm going to collect."

Sandra Marton

COLE CAMERON'S REVENGE

RED HOT REVENGE

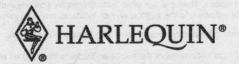

HARLEQUIN®

TORONTO • NEW YORK • LONDON
AMSTERDAM • PARIS • SYDNEY • HAMBURG
STOCKHOLM • ATHENS • TOKYO • MILAN • MADRID
PRAGUE • WARSAW • BUDAPEST • AUCKLAND

ISBN 0-373-12223-3

COLE CAMERON'S REVENGE

First North American Publication 2002.

Copyright © 2001 by Sandra Myles.

Visit us at www.eHarlequin.com

Printed in U.S.A.

PROLOGUE

Liberty, Georgia, nine years ago.

THE Cameron family had lived in Liberty for as long as anybody could recall.

First they'd farmed the land. Then they'd ranched it, and when real estate values went sky high they subdivided it and built houses. The houses weren't very good but they were big and expensive. It wasn't cheap to live in a town that was rapidly becoming an Atlanta suburb.

Nowadays, the Camerons also owned the biggest bank in Liberty, the most prosperous realty company, and there wasn't a politician in the state didn't know where to go to pick up a fat check in return for an occasional favor.

People talked about the Camerons with respect. They talked about Isaiah that way and about his eldest son, Ted...but that wasn't how they talked about Cole.

Ted spoke of his kid brother with love. Mrs. Sherry, the high school principal, talked about him with regret. Sheriff Steele talked about him with dismay.

Isaiah talked about him with disgust.

Cole didn't care. He had once, a long time ago, but by the time he was in his eighteenth summer he'd given up hoping his father would ever look at him with love, the way he looked at Ted, or even with affection, the way he looked at his dogs.

By then, Cole was little over six foot two. He had brown hair streaked gold by the sun, green eyes, and a body leanly muscled from years of working on his father's housing developments. Isaiah had never given his younger son a penny unless he worked for it.

The boy had been nothing but trouble from the day he was born.

Most of the female population of Liberty talked about Cole, too, but in whispers. They dreamed, and fantasized, and sighed, especially now that he was almost a man. He had his pick of females, all ages and sizes, and because he was young he flirted with them all and slept with the ones who were the prettiest. He never set out to hurt a woman's feelings but maybe because they were so available or maybe because he was never satisfied with the present for very long, he broke a lot of hearts. And if, once in a while, he really did get into trouble riding his secondhand Harley too fast or cutting school or maybe drinking one beer too many, it just made him all the more appealing.

Ted, who was as unlike Cole as day was from night, worried that his brother would get into serious trouble one day. Isaiah didn't worry. As far as he was concerned, it was inevitable. Cole always felt his father wouldn't mind seeing that day come and might even rejoice when it finally arrived.

"You ruined my life," Isaiah told him more than once, "the day you were born."

Cole figured it was the truth. His mother had died giving him life and nothing he could possibly do would make up for the loss.

The end came sooner than anyone anticipated, not in one definable moment but in a series of seemingly unconnected events.

Her name was Faith. Her father was a man looking for something he'd never found, either in a woman or a bottle. He drifted from town to town through the South, taking whatever work he could find and dragging Faith and her mother with him. That summer, he settled his family in a trailer on the outskirts of Liberty.

One Monday—a day Cole had decided to go to school instead of doing something more interesting—he sauntered into the cafeteria at lunchtime and his gaze swept straight past the little clutch of cheerleaders waiting on his next move, past the jocks he played with on the Liberty High football team, and settled on an angel with long, pale blond hair and cornflower-blue eyes.

Cole flashed her a devastating smile and turned on the charm that never failed him. Nothing happened. It took him a week to get Faith Davenport to smile in return, another week before she'd eat lunch with him and by the time she finally agreed to let him take her out, Cole Cameron was, in the words of the poets, well and truly smitten.

His friends thought he'd lost his mind. Faith was pretty but not beautiful; she didn't sparkle the way other girls did and she didn't treat Cole like the catch he was. Cole didn't care. There was a freshness to her, a sweetness unlike anything he'd ever known, and he felt something reach into his chest and squeeze his heart.

After their second date, Cole wanted more. Not sex: Faith was innocent, he was certain. For the first time in his life he didn't want to seduce a girl so much as he just wanted to be with her. She was easy to talk to, she was good, she was gentle…and she didn't see him as a bad-boy celebrity. He was just Cole Cameron, and she saw qualities in him he'd never known were there. Good qualities. That was a new experience.

He laughed when she told him he was smart. But he began hitting the books and the next thing he knew, he was acing his exams. School suddenly became interesting. He started showing up every day. When Faith asked where he wanted to go to college, he blinked. He wasn't planning on college but she persisted, so he had a talk with his guidance counselor and yes, it looked as if maybe, with his newly improved grades and his football skills, he might just wangle himself a scholarship because there was no way his father would foot the bill.

Faith was changing his life and Cole loved it. The truth was that he loved her. He wanted to tell her that, to ask her to go steady but before he could, he had an unpleasant duty to perform.

He'd been seeing a woman. Not a girl—a woman. She wasn't the first Liberty housewife who'd tried to seduce him but she was the first who'd succeeded. Her name was Jeanine. She was the young, sexy, bored wife of fat, middle-aged Edward Francke, who owned half the businesses and most of the politicians in town.

Cole had noticed her. Hell, every male in town over the age of ten had noticed her.

One day, when his old Harley had quit on the road to Windham Lake and he'd stripped off his shirt while he worked on it, Jeanine pulled her Cadillac onto the shoulder next to him. The late-morning sun was hot, the air humid. Cole noticed the Caddy and the woman, but he was too intent on getting the motorcycle working to pay either much attention.

Jeanine said hi. Cole said hi in return. After a couple of minutes, she got out of the car.

"You know a lot about engines?" she said in a whispery drawl.

Cole, still busy with the bike, shrugged his shoulders. "Enough to fool around some."

She gave a silvery laugh. "Well, then, how'd you like to fool around with mine?"

That was when Cole looked at her, let his eyes drift slowly up her long, bare legs, over her full bosom to her face. He'd watched her pink tongue snake slowly over her bottom lip and he'd known exactly what engine she meant.

By the time he met Faith, he'd been screwing Jeanine for a couple of months. Friday afternoons, when her husband was over in the next county playing golf, Cole would ride his bike out to her house on the lake and then ride her until they were both exhausted. It had never been as much fun as he'd hoped it would be and, after he met Faith, he stopped. Just stopped. He figured Jeanine would figure out that it was over.

He had no desire to see any female except Faith, even if it meant giving up sex, which he'd done because of Faith's innocence. It was true that their last couple of dates, things had heated up. Faith had whimpered in his arms. He'd touched her breasts. She'd even taken his hand in hers and brought it low on her belly and he'd wanted to accept that sweet invitation but he hadn't.

Faith wasn't like that. She was a fresh flower, not to be taken casually. He'd wait until he was out of school, until he had a job...until he could buy her a ring, get down on one knee and ask her to be his wife.

And then, on what would turn out to be the start of Cole's last weekend in Liberty, everything went to pieces.

Jeanine phoned him the afternoon of the Liberty High senior prom. The housekeeper gave him a funny look when she told him he had a call and Cole knew the reason the minute he heard that hoarse, sexy voice.

She had to see him, she said. It was urgent. She sounded panicked so Cole got on his Harley, rode out to her house. She was waiting for him and the "urgency" was that she hadn't seen him in weeks and weeks and where in hell had he been? Cole told her, as gently as he could, that things were over between them.

She didn't take the news well. She pouted, then she raged. At last, she threatened.

"Nobody walks out on me, Cole Cameron," she shouted as he rode off. "It's not over until I say it is. You can't just do whatever you want and get away with it!"

His father, his teachers, everybody in Cole's life had been giving him that same message for as long as he could remember. Jeanine's warning was just one more to ignore.

That night, Cole put on his rented tux, borrowed Ted's car and called for Faith. He knew she was embarrassed by the differences between the big house he'd grown up in and the trailer she lived in but he'd assured her that it didn't matter.

What he'd never told her was that his father thought it did.

When Isaiah heard the rumor that his youngest son was dating a girl from the trailer park, he'd spoken to Cole for the first time in weeks, warning him to be careful of females after the Cameron name and money.

Cole found the speech laughable considering that everybody knew he had the name but not the money. Isaiah always made it clear that he had a good son and a bad son, and that Cole would never get a dime of his money.

As it turned out, his father's speech was a warning Cole should have taken to heart.

That night, he drove to the trailer, picked up Faith. She was beautiful, almost ethereal in a gown she'd made herself of white lace and pale pink silk. He helped her into Ted's car, set off for the high school gym, but halfway there Faith reached over and put her hand on his thigh.

His skin felt as if it were burning; his breath caught in his throat.

"I don't want to go to the dance," she whispered. "Take me to the lake, Cole. To our place. Please."

Cole hesitated, though he could already feel the blood pooling in his groin. "Their place" was a grassy bank hidden among the trees where he'd touched her breasts and come as close as he'd ever been in his young life to losing control.

"Are you sure?" he finally said, in a voice so thick he hardly knew it as his own.

Faith replied by leaning over and kissing him.

He drove to the lake, took a blanket from the trunk of Ted's car and spread it on the grass. Then he undressed Faith, undressed himself, and found everything he'd ever imagined as he took the gift of her sweet virginity.

"I'm going to marry you," he whispered as she lay in his arms and she smiled, kissed his mouth and drew him deep inside her again.

He had her back at the trailer park by midnight, which was her curfew even on this special night, this prom night…this night he'd finally declared his love and made Faith his, forever. Keyed up, too high on happiness to sleep, Cole drove into the hills overlooking the town and thought about Faith and how much he loved her, and of the life they'd share.

The first rays of morning sunlight were touching the hills when he drove Ted's car back to the big house that had never felt like home. He put the car into the garage and slipped, unnoticed, into his bed. He was deep in sleep when Isaiah flung open the bedroom door.

"You worthless fool," he shouted, grabbing Cole by the arm and yanking him from the bed. "Were you drunk or are you just plain stupid?"

Baffled, half asleep, Cole blinked his eyes and stared at his father. "What's the matter?"

His father slapped his face. "Don't give me that crap, boy. You broke into the Francke's house last night."

"What?"

"You heard me. You broke into their house and trashed the living room."

"I don't know what the hell you're talking about. I wasn't anywhere near the Francke's house last night."

"Francke's wife saw you. She was on the prom committee. She saw you coming out the window just as she came home."

"I don't care what she says. She couldn't have seen me because I wasn't there."

"She says it was you, all right, and you did it because she wouldn't give you what you wanted."

"The lady says you've been sniffing around her like a dog around a bone," another voice said.

Cole looked past his father. Sheriff Steele was standing in the doorway. "That's not true, either."

"No?"

"No," Cole repeated coldly. "If anything, it's just the opposite, Sheriff. She's pissed off because I won't do what she wants."

Isaiah raised his hand to strike his son again. Cole's eyes met his father's and the older man took a step back.

"The woman says she saw you, boy."

"She's lying." Cole looked at the sheriff. "I wasn't anywhere near the Francke place last night."

"Where were you, then?"

At the prom, Cole almost said, but he saw the little glint in the sheriff's eyes.

"That's right," the sheriff said softly. "I already checked. You weren't at the dance. You weren't anywhere near the high school. Mrs. Francke would have seen you if you were. So, if you didn't go to her house and trash it, where were you?"

With Faith, down by the lake. Cole opened his mouth, then clamped it shut.

The sheriff grinned. "Cat got your tongue, son?"

Cole stared at the men. How could he tell the truth without involving Faith? The whole town would start talking, making up stories that would get wilder as they spread. And the very thought of the sheriff going to Faith for confirmation of Cole's story made his belly clench. Faith's old man was a drunk; he was mean. God only knew what he'd do if the law turned up to question his daughter.

"Answer the man," Isaiah barked.

"I said all I'm going to say. I didn't do what Mrs. Francke says I did."

"You got a way to prove that, son?"

Cole looked at the sheriff. "The only proof I can give you is my word."

"Your word," his father said, and laughed. "Your word is useless, same as you are. I don't know how I could have had two sons and one of 'em be not worth a damn."

Cole saw his brother's pinched white face appear just past his father's shoulder.

"I didn't do it," he said, as much to Ted as to anybody else.

"I know you didn't," Ted said, but it didn't matter. Things moved quickly after that. Francke had told the sheriff he wouldn't bring charges if he were paid for the items that had been smashed. The sheriff said he didn't see how anything would be gained if he locked Cole up. And Isaiah said he didn't give a damn one way or the other.

"You're not my son anymore," he said coldly. "I want you out of this house, tonight."

Cole wanted to object, not to being thrown out of Cameron House but to being found guilty, but how could he? Nobody was going to listen to him. By morning, the story would be all over town. He'd be a pariah. It was one thing to ride a motorcycle too fast or cut school, or even chug down too many beers. Breaking into a house, vandalizing it, was different.

There was only one way out of this mess.

He had to leave Liberty and not return until he'd made himself bigger than the lies Jeanine Francke had fabricated. Then he could shove the allegations down his accusers' throats, walk straight to Faith's door and claim her as his own.

He'd go to Faith, tell her what had happened, vow that he'd come back for her someday...

But how could he? Just turning up at the trailer park would

drag her into this mess. Faith, his sweet, innocent Faith, would listen to his story and insist on going straight to his father and the sheriff to defend him. And she'd be ruined. Wasn't that precisely what he was determined to avoid happening?

There was only one way to prove his love for his girl. He had to leave her and never look back. The truth was, she deserved somebody better. She always had.

The dream wasn't just over, it was dead.

"I want you out of this house, boy." Isaiah folded his arms. "You have ten minutes to pack."

Cole tossed jeans and T-shirts into a beaten-up backpack. When he'd finished, Isaiah held out a hundred-dollar bill. He took it, tore it in half and dropped it at his father's feet. Then he went out the door and away from the house that had never felt like home. He climbed onto his Harley and gunned the engine to life just as Ted ran down the steps.

"Cole," Ted hollered, "wait."

Cole had already started the bike moving. "Take care of Faith," he said.

"What should I tell her?"

That I love her, Cole thought, that I'll always love her...

"Nothing. You hear me, Teddy? Take care of her. Make sure she's okay. And—and don't tell her what happened."

"Yeah, but she'll ask."

"Let her think I got tired of it here and took off. It's better if I just get the hell out of her life."

"No. Cole, please—"

"Swear it!"

Ted sighed. "Yeah," he said, "okay. But where will you go? How will you live? Cole—"

Cole let in the clutch and roared down the driveway.

Two years later, he'd worked his way across Georgia to Corpus Christi and then across the oceans of the world on an oil tanker, to Kuwait. He'd grown up. He'd stopped being so brash. His luck started to change and he lost some of the bitterness that plagued him.

More and more, he thought about going home. About seeing Ted and maybe even somehow reconciling with his father.

Mostly, he thought about going back to claim Faith, and the life they could have together. He was in the midst of making plans to do just that when a letter arrived from Ted. The envelope was dirty and torn; it looked as if it had followed him around the world for almost as long as he'd been away.

Cole opened the envelope and read the letter inside. It said that his father was dead. He'd had a heart attack and died more than a year ago.

He waited to feel some sense of loss for the man who'd sired him but there was nothing except a small, cold disappointment that he'd been deprived of the chance to confront Isaiah and tell him how wrong he'd been about his youngest son.

Dad left everything to me, Ted wrote. *Of course, that's not the way it should be. We'll sort things out when you get home.*

Cole smiled tightly. Ted would think that way but he didn't want a penny of the Cameron money. He turned the letter over, blinked at the next line.

I don't quite know how to tell you this. Understand, I did it because of what you told me, to take care of Faith. She was so alone after you left, so desperate...

"No," Cole whispered, "no..."

His brother was married. Married to Faith, to the girl Cole loved, the girl he worshiped, the girl whose memory was all that had kept him alive while he'd struggled to find a place for himself in life. Isaiah, damn him, had been right.

I love you, she'd said, *I'll never love anyone but you...* but she'd been after the Cameron name and money all along.

The rest of the letter was a blur. Cole crumpled it in his hand; a roar of anguish ripped from his throat. Men standing near him looked up, then slowly moved away. They were roughnecks, same as he. They could handle themselves anywhere black gold oozed from the earth, but not one of them wanted to deal with what they saw in Cole Cameron's eyes that day.

He tore the letter into tiny pieces and flung them to the wind that swept endlessly across the desert sand. Then he turned his back on home, on Ted, on Faith, on everything he'd ever been stupid enough to let himself believe in or want.

From that moment on, the only thing Cole believed in was getting rich.

And the only thing he wanted was revenge.

CHAPTER ONE

Liberty, Georgia, today.

JUNE had come to Georgia, bringing with it heat so fierce it might have been midsummer. Even now, at a little before nine in the morning, the air was thick and weighted with humidity.

Faith, sitting before her dressing-table mirror, all but groaned with despair. Any other morning, she wouldn't have been bothered by the weather. She'd grown up in the South and she knew that the only way to deal with summer was to ignore it. You scraped your hair into a ponytail, put on shorts, T-shirt and sandals, and left your face scrubbed and bare.

But not today.

In just over an hour, she had a meeting with Sam Jergen, Ted's lawyer. She had to look like Faith Cameron, not Faith Davenport. Jergen didn't like her. He still thought of her as a seventeen-year-old tramp who'd trapped his client into marriage nine long years ago. She'd known that the minute she'd met him, but the lawyer wasn't stupid. He'd been careful to treat her with respect while Ted was alive.

He gave up the pretense the day of the funeral.

"Sorry for your trouble, Miz Davenport," Jergen had said as he took her hand, and then he'd smiled slyly. "Sorry about that. I meant Miz Cameron, of course."

Of course, Faith thought, tightening her jaw.

What he'd really meant to call her was one of the names the town used for her, but she hadn't given him the pleasure of reacting. She wouldn't today, either, even though she figured he'd do his best to demean her.

Tears blurred Faith's eyes.

Ted, gone.

She still couldn't believe it, that her husband had lost his life in an automobile accident on a rain-slicked back road between Liberty and Atlanta. The weeks since then had gone by in a haze. There'd been people coming and going, supposedly to offer their condolences but really, she knew, to get a first good look at her now that nobody was around to protect her from gossip.

It was old gossip, but what did that matter? Gossip could linger for a lifetime in a place like Liberty, especially when it was juicy. And what could have been more juicy than her quick trip up the altar with one Cameron brother after she'd been ditched by the other...except, maybe, the speed with which she'd become pregnant?

Faith picked up her brush and stroked it through her hair.

Oh, if only she could cancel today's meeting—but there wasn't any point in putting off what had to be done. Jergen had made it clear this was important.

"It's about your husband's estate," he'd said.

She'd almost told him to stop trying to sound so officious. What would take place this morning wasn't any surprise. This was the formal reading of Ted's will but she knew what was in it. Her practical husband had insisted on telling her the details of the document he'd suddenly decided to draw up a year ago.

He'd left everything to her, in trust for Peter. "It's his birthright," he'd said.

Faith had hesitated. "Are you sure you don't want to leave something to..." She couldn't say the name. "To your brother?"

Ted's eyes had darkened, just enough so she knew that time hadn't dulled the pain he felt. He hadn't heard from Cole since he'd sent him the letter about their marriage. Though they never talked about it, she knew he was blind to the truth; he couldn't or wouldn't see Cole for what he was, but she understood that. Love could warp your judgment. Hadn't she wept nights for Cole, even after he'd abandoned her? She, at least, had come to her senses.

"No," he'd said softly, "there's no point. Cole hated this house. He hated our father. He wouldn't want anything that

carries the Cameron name. But I know he'll come back someday, Faith. And when he does, you have to tell him the truth.
He's entitled to know he gave you a child, just as Peter has
the right to know the man who's really his father."

Faith stared into the mirror. Cole wasn't entitled to anything. Not from her. As for Peter... She couldn't imagine a
time she'd want to hurt him by telling him that his real father
had run out on her. Her child was better off going through life
thinking of Ted as his father. He'd be happy that way, and
her son's happiness was all that mattered. It was why she'd
agreed to marry Ted—and why she'd decided to leave Liberty,
as soon as the formal reading of the will was over.

This morning, after the lawyer finished with all the legal
rigmarole, she'd have the money to start life fresh and she was
going to do it in a place far from here, a place where
"Cameron" was just another name. Making the decision
hadn't been easy. Despite everything, Liberty was home. But
there was that old saying, something about home being where
the heart was.

Without Ted, this place had no heart. The sooner she left,
the better.

Faith rose from the dressing table, walked briskly to the
closet and opened it. She ran a hand along the clothing hanging from the rod, pausing when her fingers brushed over the
pink suit she'd worn for Ted's funeral. People had stared at
her openly, condemnation glittering in their eyes. The hell with
them, she'd thought. The suit was for Ted, who'd hated black.

But today wasn't about her love and respect for Ted. It was
about Peter's future. She had no idea what it took—if, in fact,
it took anything—to set in motion the things that would set
the two of them free of Liberty. She knew nothing about the
financial aspects of the life she'd lived as Mrs. Theodore
Cameron. Ted had handled all of that.

She chose a cream silk blouse, then a black silk suit. Silk,
on a day like this. She'd probably melt from the heat, but it
was the right outfit to wear. She dressed quickly, grimacing
as she pulled on panty hose, a bra, even a half-slip. The blouse
stuck to her skin almost as soon as she slipped it on but at

last she was ready, her skirt zipped, her jacket buttoned, her feet jammed into the confines of a pair of low-heeled black leather pumps.

She took a deep breath. "Ready or not," she said softly, and turned to the mirror.

The suit was fine, businesslike and purposeful, and so long as she kept the jacket buttoned nobody would know that beads of sweat were already forming beneath the blouse. The shoes were okay, too. But her hair...

"Dammit," Faith muttered.

It was reacting to the humidity the way it always did, by spinning itself into gold curls instead of lying in the soft, lady-like waves she wanted. Her face was shining, too, despite its unaccustomed dusting of powder.

So much for looking cool and confident. She looked the way she felt, uncertain and grief-stricken at the loss of the only person who'd ever truly cared for her. Perhaps, she thought wryly, the mirror was determined to reflect a portrait of the inner woman instead of the outer one.

"Mommy?"

Faith swung around. "Peter?"

Her son pushed the door open and came into the bedroom, his face solemn—too solemn for a boy his age. Her heart swelled with love at the sight of him. She squatted down and opened her arms wide. Peter walked toward her and when he was close enough, Faith reached out and drew him close, sighing as she felt the tension in his stiff body.

"Mommy? Alice says you're going to town."

Faith drew back, smiled and brushed his silky chestnut hair back from his forehead. "She's right."

"Do you have to go?"

"Yes. But I won't be long, sweetheart. Just an hour or two, I promise."

Her son nodded. He'd taken Ted's death hard. Lately, he didn't want to be away from her side.

"Would you like me to bring you something?"

Peter shook his head. "No, thank you."

"A new game from the computer store?"

"Dad bought me one, just before... He bought me one." Peter's lip quivered. "I wish he was still here, Mommy."

Faith gathered her son tightly into her embrace. "Me, too." She held him for a minute, inhaling his little-boy scent. Then she cleared her throat, cupped his shoulders and held him out in front of her. "So," she said briskly, "what are you going to do until I get home?"

Peter shrugged. "I don't know."

"How about phoning Charlie and asking him over?"

"Charlie isn't home. Today's Sean's party, remember?"

Damn, Faith thought, of course. She was so wrapped up in her own worries that she'd forgotten her son's distress at being the only boy who hadn't been asked to his classmate's party.

"Why wasn't I invited, too?" Peter had said, and she'd come within a breath of telling him the truth, that the town was already reassessing her position and his in Liberty's rigid social order.

"Because Sean's a ninny," she'd said with forced gaiety, "and besides, why would you want to go to his old party when we can have a party right here, all by ourselves?"

"It's a good thing you reminded me," Faith said. "That means today is our party, too. I'll pick up some goodies on my way home."

"Uh-huh," Peter said, with polite disinterest.

"Let's see... I'll get some liver..."

"Liv-er! Yuck. I hate liver."

"And some Brussels sprouts..."

"Double yuck!"

"Or maybe lima beans. That's it. Liver, and lima beans, and tapioca pudding for dessert—"

"The stuff with the eyeballs in it?"

"Sure. Isn't that your favorite meal?"

"No way, Mommy! Lima beans and liver and eyeball pudding isn't a party!"

"Isn't it?" Faith grinned. To her delight, her son grinned back. "Well then, I guess I'll have to pick up some yucky stuff like hamburgers and French fries and chocolate malteds at the Burger Pit."

It was a bribe, she thought a few minutes later, as she drove out the gates of the Cameron estate and turned her station wagon onto the main road, but so what? It had brought a smile to her little boy's face. His happiness was everything to her.

Ted had felt the same way.

Ted, Faith thought, and she felt the sorrow welling inside her heart again. What a wonderful man he'd been. The people of Liberty thought so, too, even if they also thought he was a fool to have married her.

Her hands tightened on the wheel. What had made him come to see her, that fateful day nine long years ago? Cole had been gone just a little over seven weeks when he'd knocked at the trailer door. Her mother had opened it, then stepped back with a little gasp.

"My word," she'd said. "You must be... Faith? It's—it's Mr. Cameron."

Faith had been in the tiny kitchen. Her heart had leaped into her throat at the sound of those words. "Cole," she'd said, "oh, Cole..."

But it was Ted she saw, when she came racing to the door. She knew him by sight, though they'd never spoken. Ted was years older than Cole. He worked in the bank his father owned. The only other thing she knew about him was that Cole said the two of them were as different as night and day.

"What do you want?" she'd said, disappointment sharpening her tone. Ted had smiled and said he'd come to see her, acting as if he made visits to trailer parks all the time, and saying, "Yes, thank you very much," to her flustered mother's offer of a cup of tea.

"Are you okay?" he'd asked quietly, once he and Faith were alone.

"I don't know what you mean."

"Look, Faith, I know you and Cole... I know he meant a lot to you—"

"Cole?" Faith tossed her head. "I hardly remember him."

"Faith. Please. I know you're hurt—"

"You don't know anything!" Without warning, she started

to weep. "I hate your brother. You hear what I'm saying? I *hate* him!"

Ted's gaze went from her face to her hand. She looked down and realized that she'd inadvertently placed her hand protectively over her still-flat stomach. Heat rushed to her face as she looked up and her eyes met Ted's.

"You're pregnant," he said softly.

"No!" Her face turned white. "I'm not...pregnant," she said, the word hissing softly from between her teeth. She shot a nervous glance over her shoulder. "You go home, you hear me? Just—just get out of here and—"

"Don't lie to me, dammit. You're carrying my brother's child."

The fight went out of her like air from a collapsing balloon. She sank down on the stained sofa and he sat down beside her, his eyes never leaving hers.

"What are you going to do?"

"Keep your voice down!"

"Faith." Ted took her hand. "You have to tell me what you're going to do."

"I'm not getting rid of my baby," she said, jerking her hand from his, "if that's what you were thinking."

"I don't know what I'm thinking," he said honestly. "Aren't you still in high school?"

"So?"

"So, how can you hope to take care of a baby?"

"I'll do what I have to do."

"Meaning, you'll quit school, take a job at the Burger Pit, have your baby and bring him home to this place."

Faith felt her cheeks flame. "'This place,'" she said, trying to sound offended but knowing she probably only sounded defensive, "is my home."

Ted was blunt. "Sure," he said, "and that's what you want for your baby, right? And for yourself?"

How she'd despised him that day! He'd forced her to see that cramped, ugly little room; to smell the stink of beer rising from the sagging furniture; to hear her father's snores coming through the pressboard walls while he slept off a drunk.

Cole used to hold her in his arms and tell her he'd take her away from all this someday but Cole had lied. Now she sat beside his brother while he told her, in painfully bleak terms, that she'd never escape this life, that, worse still, her child would never escape it.

"Let me help you, Faith."

"I don't want Cameron charity."

"I'm not talking about charity, I'm talking about doing the right thing for Cole's child. What are you going to tell people, when they see that you're pregnant?"

"I don't have to tell them anything," she said, even though it was a lie. Liberty wasn't the kind of town where you could tell people to mind their own business.

"You mean, you'd rather keep your pride and let people play guessing games about who put that baby inside you?"

"They'll do that anyway."

Ted shifted closer to her. She could still remember the sound of the ancient springs in the sofa creaking as he did.

"You're right," he said softly. "That's why I'm not offering you money."

"Well, that's something. I meant it when I said—"

"I want you to marry me, Faith."

She'd gaped at him, certain he'd lost his mind. "Marry you?"

"That's right."

"Are you crazy? I don't want to marry you. I don't love you. I don't even know you."

"That makes two of us. I don't love you or know you and, frankly, I don't want to marry you, either."

"Then, why…"

"For the child, that's why. You owe him a decent life." Ted took a long, dismissive look around the trailer before locking eyes with her again. "Unless you prefer this."

"I grew up just fine without your big house and all your money," she replied fiercely.

"Yes," Ted said, "you did. But don't you want your child to have more? Don't you want him to be legitimate?" He leaned forward, reached for her hand. "Tell me you love that baby enough to let me do the right thing for you both."

"You think what you're suggesting is the right thing?" Faith tried to tug her hand from his again but he wouldn't let her. "I'd sooner marry the devil than marry a Cameron."

Thinking back, she knew she hadn't quite pulled it off. Her words had tried for bravado but her voice had quavered with despair.

"Cole asked me to look after you," Ted said quietly.

To this day, she hated herself for the way her foolish heart had jumped at those words.

"Did he?" she whispered, then answered her own question. "No. No, he didn't. Cole doesn't give a damn about me. He proved it by leaving without so much as a goodbye. He never even tried to get in touch with me, right after the night we'd— the night we'd—"

"Faith." Ted stood up. "My brother did what he had to do."

"Oh, yes," she said, rising to her feet. She gave a quick laugh. "He certainly did."

"And so will you, if you're half the woman I think you are. You'll marry me, take the Cameron name, raise your baby as a Cameron—"

"And what about you?" She stared at Ted in bewilderment. "Assuming I were to agree to such an insane thing—which I won't—but if I did, what would happen to your life? I—I'd never live with you as a wife should. Never, no matter how—"

"I know that. And I wouldn't expect it." Ted cleared his throat. "I'm going to... I'm going to trust you with something. Something you should know." He swallowed hard. "I've— I've never been interested in women. Not the way a man should be."

The truth took a long moment to sink in. When it finally did, Faith stared at him, speechless.

"Nobody knows," he'd said quickly, "not even Cole. And nobody ever will, not in Liberty. I'll be an exemplary husband. And, I promise you, I'll love Cole's child as if it were my own. Just don't make this baby pay for what you feel toward my brother."

"I hate your brother," she'd said, and despite everything, the enormity of the lie had clutched at her heart.

"But you don't hate your baby." Ted had flashed the gentle smile she'd come to know so well over the ensuing years. "You'll be doing me a favor, letting me enjoy a child I'd never otherwise have. No, don't say anything. At least agree to think it over."

She'd thought it over, trying to concentrate on the logic of it instead of on the pain of her broken heart. Then, one morning her mother found her retching into the toilet. She whispered the question Faith had feared for weeks, and Faith nodded her assent.

"Your father mustn't know," her mother had said, trembling. "You'll have to do something, Faith, but not in this town. You'll have to do it far away from here."

A day later, she'd phoned Ted and accepted his proposition.

They'd been married at Town Hall while her mother stood by sniffling into a fistful of tissues. Ted put a thin platinum band on her finger, kissed her cheek and moved her into his house. He sent Cole a letter telling him about the marriage, but Cole never replied. And Isaiah never said a word to her, right up until his death.

Neither did anyone else in town, but she saw their knowing smiles. When she began to show, their smiles grew more obvious. She knew people were counting the months and assuming she'd managed to snare a Cameron in the oldest way possible.

"Don't mind those busybodies," Ted would say when she'd come home from the market or the library with her face red and her temper high. "Just go on with your life."

She had. And, once Peter was born, her days were filled with the sweet joy of caring for him. He was the love of her life, the one good thing Cole had given her, and when Ted suggested finding Cole to tell him he had a son, Faith's "no" was adamant. Cole hadn't wanted her; why would he want to know he had a son?

"I don't ever want him to know about Peter," she'd said. "Promise me that, Ted."

Ted had promised, though reluctantly. "It's wrong," he'd say. "A man has the right to know he's a father."

Now, turning onto Main Street and pulling into the lot behind Sam Jergen's law office, Faith thought again, as she had so often in the past, that fathering a child was easy. Raising one was the hard part although the truth was, Ted hadn't been all that involved in raising Peter. He had his own life but he'd always been good to her and to her son. Thanks to that goodness, she could look forward to a fresh start for the two of them.

Damn. There was a car, a shiny black Jaguar, parked under the only shade tree. It gave her a jolt to see it, considering the memories swirling through her head. When Cole daydreamed about their future, he used to say that someday he'd trade his Harley for a Jaguar...

She shut off the engine.

Why was she wasting time thinking about Cole this morning? The past was dead. The future was all that mattered.

The day was heating up. She could feel the asphalt give under her shoes as she walked across the parking lot. A merciful blast of frigid air enveloped her as she stepped inside the marble foyer of the old building. Five to nine, said the big clock on the wall. She was right on time.

The cool air evaporated as she made her way up the steps to the third floor and down the corridor to Sam Jergen's office. Faith could feel her hair curling, her blouse wilting. She paused outside the office, wiped her hand down her skirt, tugged at her jacket, patted her hair...

"Just stop it," she said under her breath, and she opened the door and stepped inside.

The empty reception area was hot, almost airless. Faith glanced at her watch. It was precisely nine o'clock. Where was the iron-jawed secretary who normally sat at the desk?

"Hello?" she said, after a couple of minutes crept past.

There was no reply. Faith sat down on the sofa, put her

purse in her lap and folded her hands over it. She looked at her watch again, frowned and got to her feet.

"Hello?" she said again, in a louder voice.

A sound drifted down the short corridor that led to the inner offices. Laughter? Yes, that was what it was, a peal of feminine laughter. Faith looked around, huffed out a breath and started down the hall.

She could hear voices now, though she couldn't make out the words. A man and a woman were talking. The woman was Jergen's secretary. Faith had spoken with her enough times lately to know that. But the man wasn't Sam Jergen. He was younger, and his voice was deeper, huskier, maybe even a little sexy...

Goose bumps prickled her arms under the silk blouse. She jerked to a stop. Something in the way the man sounded was familiar.

The woman laughed again, and so did the man. Faith began to tremble. She turned on her heel, started back down the corridor. Obviously, she'd made a mistake. Come on the wrong day, maybe, or at the wrong time...

"Mrs. Cameron?"

Whatever, she'd go home, call and ask when she was supposed to have shown up for this meeting...

"Mrs. Cameron?"

Faith stumbled to a halt. She was breathing hard and her pulse was racing, which was silly.

"Yes?" she said brightly, and turned toward the secretary. "I'm awfully sorry to have bothered you. I'm afraid I've showed up at the wrong—" The other woman was looking at her as if she'd lost her mind. "Actually, I—I just remembered something I have to—to—"

Faith fell silent. The open door to Jergen's private office was just ahead. She could see a man standing near the windows. He was tall, well over six feet; his hair was a sun-streaked brown, perhaps a little longer than it should have been, and curled just over his collar. He was wearing a pale gray suit that surely had been tailored to his wide-shouldered, leanly muscled frame. His feet were slightly spread and his hands were in his trouser pockets.

His stance was casual but something about it suggested that he knew he owned the world.

Faith's heartbeat slowed to a sluggish crawl. She forced her eyes from the man to Jergen's secretary.

"Why don't I come back later?" she said in a breathless voice that didn't sound a bit like her own. "Say, at ten? Or this afternoon? I mean, I thought I had a nine o'clock appointment but obviously—"

"You do. Mr. Jergen had to step out for a minute. He asked you to wait for him in his office."

"No! I can wait in the reception area—"

The woman took her arm. Faith wanted to grab for the wall and hang on but the secretary drew her forward, through the door and into the office.

"No," she said again, but it was too late. The man turned from the window and looked at her.

"Hello, Faith," Cole said.

And everything went black.

CHAPTER TWO

COLE had wondered how Faith would react when she saw him.

He'd thought about it through the long flight home—not that Georgia was home anymore. He had offices in Caracas, London and New York, a condo in Aspen and a penthouse in New York but when the news of Ted's death reached him, he was deep in the Orinoco basin. It had taken him more than a week just to get back to civilization.

She was such a clever actress. Who knew what routine she'd try and pull?

He'd imagined her offering a cool smile and a handshake.

Hello, Cole, she'd say, as if he'd never left. As if there'd never been anything between them. As if they'd never made love on a soft summer night.

Or she might try the ingénue act again. He'd fallen for it years ago. So had his brother. Why wouldn't she stick with something that had been successful? Sweet Faith. Innocent Faith. Oh yeah. That had always worked.

Maybe she'd play the grieving widow. Stare at him through big eyes, weep as if her heart were breaking. Actually, he'd doubted she'd be foolish enough to try that. She had to realize that he, of all men, would know she didn't have a heart.

A swoon was the last thing he'd figured but that was exactly what she did. Looked at him, rolled up her eyes and went down in a heap. Cole cursed, moved fast, and caught her just before she hit the floor.

"Get some cold water," he snapped at Sam Jergen's secretary.

The woman flew down the hall. Cole headed in the other direction, elbowed open the conference room door and unceremoniously deposited Faith on the couch. He looked at her dispassionately and wondered if he might have walked past her on the street. The girl he'd known had lived her life in shorts and T-shirts. The woman he was looking at was dressed in designer silk.

"I suppose you know all about your brother's marriage," Jergen had said carefully, when the call had finally reached him. "That he and Faith Davenport..."

"Yes," Cole had said, interrupting the man. Surely, the lawyer hadn't phoned to give him old news. "I know all of that. Why are you calling me, Mr. Jergen?"

There'd been a long silence over the satellite phone. "Your brother's been in an accident," Jergen had finally said. "I'm afraid it was a bad one. He was driving to Atlanta. It was dark and the rain was heavy..."

It was funny, what adversity could do to a man. Nine years of rage had disappeared in a heartbeat. This was Ted, his brother. And Cole loved him.

"What hospital is he in?" he'd demanded, glancing at his watch. "I can be in the States by—"

"He's not in a hospital," Jergen had said softly. "He's gone."

Ted, gone? That couldn't be. "No," Cole had whispered, "God, no..." And then his heart had almost stopped beating. "Faith? Is she...?" His hand had tightened around the phone. "Tell me what happened to her. Is she—did she—"

"She's fine," Jergen had replied, and then his voice flattened and he said that Faith hadn't been in the car. "Ted made the trip to Atlanta once a month and he always made it alone."

"Always alone? What's that supposed to mean?"

"We can talk about all of that when you get here," the lawyer had said.

"We'll talk about it now," Cole had said coldly, and, finally Jergen had obliged.

"Your brother was seeing somebody on the side," he'd said bluntly. "Nobody faulted him for it. That wife of his was cold as ice. She never showed him the, uh, the warmth a man's entitled to in a marriage."

Jergen told him about the separate bedrooms, about the lack of outward affection between Faith and his brother. Ted's housekeeper had found the situation appalling and hadn't hesitated to describe it to practically everyone in town.

"That sister-in-law of yours is some piece of work," Sam Jergen had continued. "Hooked your brother by getting him to think he'd put a bun in the oven."

"You mean, she said she was pregnant?"

"Come on, Cole. You don't think your brother would have married her otherwise, do you? Then, after she was elbow-deep in Cameron money, she showed him just what she thought of him."

"He had her sign a prenup, didn't he?"

Jergen had laughed. "Woman got him to the altar in the first place by doing away with your brother's ability to think. No, there wasn't a prenuptial agreement. Worse still, he wrote a will leaving her everything. Well, you get the house but all the rest is hers."

"Wills can be broken," Cole had said with grim determination.

He'd come to Liberty to do just that. He knew he shouldn't have hated Ted for marrying Faith. She was the one; she'd played them both for fools and now, she thought it was payoff time.

No way.

Faith had never been fit to be Ted's wife. She wasn't fit to be his widow. And that meant she sure as hell wasn't fit to claim a dime of Ted's estate. He'd fight her for every penny, win and give it to charity. Burn it. Anything, rather than see his brother's widow get her hands on the money—and she probably knew it. No wonder she'd fainted at the sight of him.

She was still lying on the couch where he'd put her, as limp as a rag doll.

Jergen's secretary skidded into the conference room, holding a tall glass of iced water and a wet towel.

"Is there anything else I can do, Mr. Cameron?"

Cole shook his head. "The lady fainted, that's all."

"Shouldn't she have come around by now?"

He squatted down beside the couch. He was wondering the same thing. Faith's face was shockingly white; he could see the swift beat of her pulse in her throat. Sweat beaded on her forehead. He looked at the heavy black silk suit and the cream-colored blouse, and muttered an oath under his breath.

"Damned fool woman, to dress like a nun on a day as hot as this."

Somewhere in the outer office, a telephone rang and rang. "The phone," Jergen's secretary blurted.

Faith moaned softly.

"She's coming around now. Go on. Do whatever you have to do. I'll deal with this." Cole wiped Faith's face with the wet cloth as Jergen's secretary shut the door behind her. "Faith." He leaned closer. "Faith, open your eyes."

Color was stealing back into her face. Cole hesitated, then began unbuttoning her jacket. He undid the top buttons of the blouse, too. Then he slipped his arm beneath her shoulders, lifted her toward him and worked the jacket off. She sighed and her head fell against his shoulder.

He felt the whisper of her breath against his throat and suddenly he remembered the last time he'd held her like this. It was the night they'd made love. Afterward, she lay curled in the curve of his arm, her breath warming his skin.

Abruptly, he pulled his arm out from under her and she fell back against the cushions.

"Faith," he said sharply, "come on, Faith. If this is for my benefit..."

Cole's voice faded away. Why had he opened her jacket? The blouse clung damply to her flesh. He could see the soft, lacy outline of her bra. In the old days, her bras had been plain white cotton but then, she hadn't needed adornment. She was all the adornment a man could take. The first time he'd un-hooked her bra, the roundness of her breasts, the soft pink of her nipples, had almost made him lose control.

All these years, and suddenly he could remember the feel of her silky flesh in his palms, the taste of it on his tongue...

Dammit.

Cole shot to his feet. What the hell was he doing? He'd hated this woman far longer than he'd wanted her. She'd lied, cheated, seduced him and then Ted. She was the reason his brother had died on a rain-slick road and yet here he was, remembering things that had been lies…and turning hard as a rock, just the same.

No wonder she'd trapped Ted in her web. He'd have been pathetically easy, smart when it came to books and numbers but naive about women, shy to the point of avoidance. What chance would the poor bastard have had when a woman with the face of an angel and the instincts of a whore turned her wiles on him?

"Faith," he said sharply, and as he did, she opened her eyes. They were blank at first but when they focused on him he saw fear splinter in their blue depths. She was right to be afraid, Cole thought, and shot her a quick, mocking smile. "Nice to see you again, baby. But you didn't have to give me such a memorable welcome."

Faith struggled to sit up. She moved too fast and the color began to seep from her face. Cole eased her back against the cushions. He didn't want her to faint again. How could he enjoy what was coming if she ended up playing the scene like a heroine in a Victorian melodrama?

"Take it easy or you'll black out again."

"Black out?"

Her voice was small and shaky. Another minute, she'd have him feeling sorry for her.

"Yeah." He took the glass from the table and handed it to her. "Black out, as in faint. Here. Drink this."

"What is it?" she said, giving the liquid a wary look.

"Water." Another quick smile that wasn't quite a smile curved his mouth. "Arsenic's too easy to trace."

Anger flickered across her face like heat lightning and disappeared as quickly. She took the glass and drank half of the contents.

"Thank you," she said stiffly.

"Don't thank me, thank Sam's secretary." Cole folded his arms. "Do you want a doctor?"

Faith shook her head. A mistake, she knew, as soon as she did it. The room whirled but she sat up anyway, swung her feet to the floor and put the glass on the table.

"I'm fine," she lied.

"There's a damp towel, too, if you want it."

"I said, I'm fine."

She wasn't. And she didn't want a damp towel, she wanted to get on her feet. Cole would still tower over her but at least that would take away some of his advantage. She just didn't know if she could manage that without falling down again— and yet, why was she so surprised to see him? Her husband was dead. Cole hadn't bothered returning for the funeral but this was different. This was all about the disposition of the Cameron estate.

A sense of unease inched the length of her spine. Would he fight her for the money? Ted had been convinced Cole wouldn't want it. She didn't want it, either. She'd told Ted that but he'd said that money belonged to Peter. To her son. Her son, and Cole's...

Cole's son.

Oh, God.

She'd stopped thinking of Peter that way years ago, but here was a walking, talking reminder of the truth. She saw a copy of her son's eyes in Cole's face, the same hair falling over Cole's forehead. Her son was only a little boy but already, he held his head the way Cole did. And there was the same tiny indentation in his chin, that same fullness to his mouth...

"Put your head down."

"I'm—I'm fine."

"The hell you are," Cole said sharply. "Put your head down and take a couple of deep breaths."

Gradually, the room stopped spinning. She lifted her head slowly. Cole was squatting in front of her, his hands cupping her shoulders.

"Are you all right?"

"Yes." She pulled back. "What are you doing here, Cole?"

Slowly, he rose to his feet. "Making women swoon at the sight of me," he said, with a cool smile.

"It's the heat."

"Yeah, well, that's what happens when you wear black on

a hot day. Or am I supposed to think you're in mourning for my brother?" His mouth thinned. "The way I hear it, you wore pink to his funeral."

"What would you know about it? You didn't even bother coming home."

"I didn't know Ted was—that there'd been an accident until weeks after it happened."

"No, of course not."

"It's the truth, dammit! I was in the field and..."

And Jergen's message had to find him, first, but why tell that to Faith? He didn't owe her anything but what she deserved.

"...and whatever scheme you were up to then was more important." Faith stood up. The floor tilted slightly and she gave herself time to recover by smoothing down her skirt. "Not that it matters now."

"Oh, it matters." Cole folded his arms over his chest. "After all, today's payoff time."

"Payoff time?"

"Sure. Finding out how much the Cameron estate is worth." His smile was all teeth. "Big doings, huh, baby?"

"And that's the reason you showed up, isn't it? To stake your claim?"

"Yes. Exactly. I'm here to claim what's mine." He let his eyes move over her with slow insolence. "You might want to button your jacket before we meet with Sam Jergen."

She looked down at herself, then at him. He saw the soft rush of pink rise to her cheeks and he gave her a slow, knowing smile.

"I opened it after you passed out. You were warm. Warm, and wet." Deliberately, he dropped his voice to a whisper. "That's what you were always best at, baby. Being warm and wet for me."

She bunched her hands into fists and he knew she wanted to hit him but she wasn't a fool. This was her big moment. Faith wasn't going to show what she was all about this morning. He saw her fingers shake as she closed the buttons but when she spoke, she sounded calm.

"It's difficult to believe you and Ted were brothers. He was a gentleman."

"That's why you were able to fool him into marrying you."

The cool facade dented. "I didn't fool him into anything."

"Sure you did." Cole caught her wrist as she started past him. "I'd never have fallen for that trick."

"Let go of me, please."

"It's the oldest game in the world."

"Let go, Cole."

"Telling a man he's made you pregnant—"

Faith swung toward him. "That's not the way it was!"

"—and after he's done the right thing, married you and given you his name, you bat your eyes and say, whoops, sorry, I made a minor miscalculation—"

"What?"

"But Ted was a good guy. He was too decent to say, okay, the joke's over and I want a divorce."

She stared at Cole in amazement. Yes, she'd made Ted promise not to tell Cole about her child but was it possible he still didn't know?

" 'Pregnant? Let me see a lab test,' another guy would have said, but not Ted. How'd you work it, Faith? It couldn't have been easy, first luring him into bed, then making him think you were having his baby—"

"Damn you! You know it all, don't you?" Her voice trembled with rage; her eyes glittered with it. "But that's not the way it was. I didn't…" Faith stopped herself in midsentence. Why tell him more than she had to? "He said—he wanted to marry me."

Cole's hand tightened on her wrist. "What'd you think, huh? That maybe my old man would change his mind about a slut like you if he thought Ted was going to give him a grandson?"

"Let go of me!"

"You can't run away, Faith. Not yet." Cole grinned. "It's payoff time, remember? The will. Don't you want to know what you're getting?"

She wrenched her hand free and this time he let her. "I hate to disappoint you," she said softly, "but I already know. Ted told me."

"Did he," he said, but she knew it wasn't a question.

"I never wanted the Cameron money."

"Of course not." Cole's eyes narrowed. "Money wasn't why you married my brother."

I married your brother because I was pregnant with your child. The words were on the tip of her tongue but Cole would never know that. He never had to know she had a child at all. All she had to do was get through the next hour. He'd leave Liberty and she'd never have to see him again.

"Believe what you like," she said. "It doesn't matter to me. Nothing about you matters to me. I came here to see Sam Jergen, not to be insulted."

Cole could feel his anger growing. She was playing at being a lady. She looked the part, even sounded it, but he knew exactly what she was.

"Damn you," he growled, grabbing her shoulders and pushing her back against the wall. "The worst part of this is trying to figure out how the hell Ted and I could have been such fools."

"Take your hands off me!"

"There was a time you wanted my hands all over you."

"Stop it."

"What's the problem, baby? Don't you like being reminded of how things used to be?"

"You—you bastard!"

Cole laughed. "Scratch the surface and find the truth. The lady bit is only skin deep."

"Let go of me. Let go, or so help me, I'll—"

"What? What will you do?"

His hands slid from her shoulders to her wrists. She winced and he knew he was hurting her but he didn't care. She'd hurt him far worse, not that it mattered anymore. He'd been over her for a long time, purged himself of the memory of her scent and taste in the arms of a hundred other women. What he couldn't get past was knowing that she'd made him hate his brother for so many years, and for what? There wasn't a way in hell she'd ever been worth the pain she'd caused.

"What did you figure, Faith? That maybe, if you were lucky, I'd never come back? That way, you'd get it all. The name, the money..."

She was crying now, tears he knew were supposed to melt his heart and turn him to clay in her hands. She'd wept in his arms that night he'd made love to her.

"Don't, sweetheart," he'd whispered, feeling clumsy and helpless, afraid he'd hurt her, and she'd kissed him and said she was crying because she was so happy, because of how it felt to belong to him, at last.

"I didn't want any of it. Not the name, not the money..."

"Sure you didn't." Cole clasped her face, forced it up to his. "You married my brother because you fell head over heels in love with him. Oh, yeah. I'll just bet you did."

"I told you. I don't give a damn what you believe—"

"Did you sleep with him right away? Or did you tease him, the way you teased me?" He gave a quick laugh. "You were some actress, baby. You had me thinking that waiting was my idea, not yours."

"I was a fool to have gotten involved with you. Everybody said you were no good. I should have believed them!"

"That's why you and I made such a good pair. Neither of us was worth a damn."

"I hate you, Cole Cameron. And I'm glad you came back because I've waited years and years to tell you that. I hate you, hate you, hate—"

Cole drove his hands into her hair, knotted the silky curls in his fingers. "That's not what you said that last night."

"Don't do this. Don't—"

"'Touch me,' you said. 'Kiss me,' you said. 'Make love to me,' you said—"

"I was young." She was panting now, struggling wildly against him, conscious of the hardness and strength of his body, of his scent, his heat. "And I was foolish. I thought you were special, that you—"

"You thought I was your ticket out. Tell me, were you

really a virgin, Faith? Or was it all make-believe, the way you blushed as I undressed you, the way you trembled in my arms?"

"I wish I'd never met you. I wish—"

"You were good, I'll give you that." His arms went around her and he pulled her tightly against him so that she could feel what she'd done to him. It was her fault that even the memory of that night could still turn him hard as stone. "You on your back, me inside you—" His gaze dropped to her parted lips, then lifted to her eyes. "Do you remember, Faith? How it felt when I moved against you? How it was to taste yourself on my mouth?"

A sob broke from her throat. "I hope there's a special place in hell for you."

"There probably is. And you can bet you'll be there with me." His hands tightened in her hair and he urged her head up. "Faith," he said thickly, and suddenly it was that night all over again, he could feel the need twisting inside him, feel the heat building in his blood...

Dammit! What was he doing? Cole let go of her, swung away, opened the door—and almost walked into Sam Jergen.

"There you are," the lawyer said. "You folks all right? My secretary said..." His voice faded as he looked from Cole to Faith. "Well," he said, and cleared his throat, "maybe we ought to take a break for a minute or two."

"No," Cole said.

"No," Faith said, in the same breath. "Just get this over with." She turned toward Jergen. Her heart felt as if it were trying to beat its way out of her breast but she forced a polite smile to her lips. "You should have told me we weren't going to be meeting alone."

"The will concerns you both, Mrs. Cameron. I thought it would save time if we discussed the provisions together."

"Discuss them, then, but this is all a technicality. I'm familiar with the terms of my late husband's will."

"I see." Jergen ran a finger under his collar. "All its terms?"

"Of course."

The lawyer heaved a relieved sigh. "Well, that disposes of that. But there are other factors..."

"What other factors?" She thought of Peter, waiting at home. "I have things to do."

"What she means," Cole said lazily, "is she wants to know exactly how much she inherits." He smiled. "Am I right?"

"Okay. That's it." Faith headed toward the door. She knew she was making a mistake, letting her emotions take over, but too much was happening. The shock of seeing Cole again. The anger he could still stir in her. His conceit in thinking he could still make her respond to him...and the horror of knowing that maybe, oh maybe, he was right. "Seeing us together may have suited you, Mr. Jergen, but I don't want any part of it. You can call me when you're free."

"From bereaved widow to outraged client." Cole clapped his hands in slow cadence. "What a performance."

She whirled toward him. "Listen, you no good son of a—"

"Mrs. Cameron. Mr. Cameron." Jergen held up his hands. "Please. Calm down."

"The lady's in a hurry, Sam." Cole looked at Faith. He was still smiling, but what she saw in his eyes made her breath catch. "So let's cut to the bottom line. Hold off on counting your money, baby."

"You're insulting, do you know that?"

"You're not getting it. Not one penny." He folded his arms, rocked back a little on his heels. "I intend to fight my brother's will in court."

Faith stared at the man she'd once thought she loved, the man she hated with every bone in her body. You don't have to fight it, she wanted to say. You can have the money, every cent... But there was Peter to consider, and the new life she had to make for him.

"Mr. Jergen?" she said softly, her eyes locked to Cole's face. "Can he do that?"

"He can do whatever he wishes, Mrs. Cameron. But—"

"Forget the 'but,' Jergen." Cole unfolded his arms and came slowly toward her. She wanted to back away but she knew what a mistake it would be to show him any sign of weakness. "I'm going to fight it, and I don't care if it means the estate is tied up in litigation forever. That would suit me just fine. Watching you spend whatever money you already stole on court battles for the next umpteen years would be a pleasure."

"Mr. Cameron. Please. If you'd let me speak—"

"Jergen, when I want your legal advice..." Cole let out a breath. "All right. What is it?"

The lawyer looked from one of them to the other. "There's nothing to fight in court," he said softly. "What I've been trying to tell you is that there isn't any money left to inherit."

CHAPTER THREE

FAITH stared at Sam Jergen. He had his finger inside his shirt collar again and from the look on his face, she knew he wanted to be anywhere but in this office.

"I don't understand," she said carefully. "What do you mean, there's no money?"

"I mean exactly what I said, Mrs. Cameron. The money is gone. Well, unless you want to count maybe two thousand dollars that's in your husband's checking account..."

"That's impossible!" Cole's voice was whip-sharp. "You've made a mistake."

"I wish I had. Unfortunately, the facts speak for themselves." Jergen lifted a large file box from the floor and placed it on the conference table. "Here are all Ted's bank and brokerage statements. I've been through them I don't know how many times, alone at first and then with an accountant. Your brother's accountant, in fact. You're more than welcome to have your people go through the documents, too."

Faith looked at Cole. His people? As stunned as she was, that almost made her laugh. Such a lofty phrase for a man who'd left town on a motorcycle and had probably returned on the bus, and never mind the expensive-looking suit. For all she knew, he'd talked some woman into buying it for him. Those were the only "people" he'd have dancing attendance on him.

"They can work here," Jergen said, holding out his arms in a gesture that made it clear he was offering the entire suite of offices. "Naturally, I'll put my staff at your disposal."

"Yes," Cole said. His voice was low, filled with authority as well as warning. "You will. But I want answers now."

The lawyer's string tie rode up and down as he swallowed. "Well, it's a complicated story, sir..."

"Simplify it, then." Cole's smile was quick and chill. "You can do that, can't you?"

Jergen blanched. "Yes. Certainly, sir."

Sir? Faith looked from one man to the other. What was going on here? She was the sole beneficiary to Ted's estate but Sam Jergen was treating Cole with deference and ignoring her. That was how it had gone since he'd entered the office.

"Unless you know the answer, my sweet sister-in-law."

It took a few seconds before she realized Cole was talking to her. She looked at him. "Answer to what?" She blinked. "Are you asking me about the money?"

He leaned toward her, that chilly smile angling across his mouth again, and slapped his hands down on either side of the file box. The sounds, flat as gunshots, startled her, and she jerked back.

"That's right," he said softly, "I'm asking you, Faith. What happened?"

"How would I know? Ted handled the accounts. I didn't have anything to do with those things."

"You make it sound as if you weren't interested in 'those things,' but we both know how wrong that is." Cole narrowed his eyes at her. "You've had plenty of time to get your hands on my brother's funds."

"Are you accusing me of theft?"

"I'm accusing you of being one clever piece of work, baby. If you've been playing games with Ted's money—"

"Your money. Isn't that what you mean? You just said you were going to fight me in court."

"Damn right, as soon as I figure out how you did this."

"Well," Jergen said cautiously, "that's not exactly—"

"Stay out of this, Jergen. This is a private matter."

"But—but..." Jergen cleared his throat. "You're wrong, sir. Mrs. Cameron had no involvement in what happened."

Cole stood up straight and folded his arms over his chest. "Prove it."

"If you'll just look at this..." The lawyer plucked a folder from the file case. Cole snatched it from him and began reading.

"I'm the one you should explain things to," Faith started to say, but when she saw the look that transformed Cole's face, her anger faded. "What is that?" she said softly.

Cole shook his head, went on reading. Then, slowly, he raised his head and stared at the attorney.

"What the hell…?"

"I know," Jergen muttered. "Incredible, isn't it?"

"What?" Faith said. "What's incredible?"

Neither man answered. Jergen folded his hands behind him and rose up and down on his toes. Cole walked to the window and tilted the folder into the sunlight, as if that might help him make better sense out of the pages inside it.

"Why?" He swung toward the lawyer. "Jergen? Explain it to me."

"I can't, sir. All I can do is show you the dates and the figures but if you mean, explain how your brother got himself into such a mess… I can't do that."

"What are you talking about?" Faith stared from one man to the other. She knew they'd all but forgotten her existence just as she knew that whatever was happening in this office threatened all her dreams for Peter's happiness. "What's in that folder, Mr. Jergen?"

"It's rather complicated, Mrs. Cameron. All you need to know is—"

"All *you* need to know," she said calmly, even though she was trembling inside, "is that taking that tone with me is a mistake. I am your client. You work for me, not for Cole Cameron, or have you forgotten that?" She strode to Cole and grabbed the folder. She expected resistance but he let her take it, even smiled a little when she did.

"Read it and weep, baby."

She opened the folder and stared blindly at the first page. Out of the corner of her eye she saw Cole hitch a hip onto the window ledge and fold his arms. He looked amused, as if what was about to happen would be entertaining. She wanted to fling something in his arrogant face. Everything in her yearned to tell him what he could do with the folder as well as the money but that was her pride whispering in her ear and pride meant nothing. It hadn't, not for years.

Peter was the only thing that mattered. Thinking of him, concentrating on how much she loved him, gave her the focus she needed. Faith stared at the page until it stopped being a blur. Columns of numbers jumped out at her. Purchases. Sales. Balances. It went on for page after page, the balances getting smaller and smaller, the accounts closing down. Finally, she looked up, seeking help from Jergen, but Cole had moved. He was standing directly in front of her, and his frigid eyes locked onto hers.

"Cole?" She held the papers out toward him. Her hand trembled. "What is this?"

"Your future," he said, almost gently. "Look at the last line."

She did. Total balance, seven hundred eighty-two dollars and...

"Those are your assets, darling." His voice was a purr. "The payoff. Not quite what you'd been expecting, is it?"

He was standing too close, invading her space. She knew it was deliberate, that he meant to throw her off balance, and he was succeeding. She didn't like having him so near, didn't want to smell the scent of his cologne, something elusive that went with the expensive suit. Tiny lines radiated out from the corners of his eyes. The years had bruised him, as she knew they'd bruised her. She was worn down by gossip, exhausted by deceitful slurs but he—he had become harder and more dangerously masculine than ever, watching her with a little smile she longed to slap from his face.

A chill raced through her blood. She took a step back and fought to keep her tone steady.

"I'd like an explanation, Mr. Jergen. Is this supposed to be all that remains of my husband's estate?"

"Late husband," Cole said. "Ted's not around to play your games anymore."

"Mr. Jergen," Faith said, ignoring Cole, "surely there are other assets. What happened to them?"

"It's complicated." Jergen patted her arm. "That's what I'm trying to tell you, Faith—"

"Then simplify it," she said, jerking away from him. "And please remember that my name is Mrs. Cameron."

She heard Cole laugh but she didn't care. She was tired of being patronized and she kept her eyes on the lawyer until he flushed.

"As you wish, Mrs. Cameron. In brief, your husband lost everything in the market."

"What market? Stocks, you mean? But Ted wasn't a gambler."

"No. He was a prudent investor—at least, he was until a couple of years ago. Then he began buying technology IPOs. Initial public offerings, Mrs. Cameron, in a sector where people were making fortunes overnight."

"Go on." Faith folded her arms. Maybe that would keep anyone from noticing that her heart was trying to pound its way out of her chest. "He invested lots of money and made lots of money. What's wrong with that?"

"Nothing, if your stocks keep escalating in value, or if you sell out in time. Your late husband made some errors in judgment. His stocks fell, but he kept buying. I suppose he thought he'd recoup. And—"

"And," Cole said, "he didn't."

Jergen smiled with gratitude. "Exactly. These papers tell the story. A few months ago, Ted sold the bank and the realty company. He'd already disposed of the construction firm. He used an attorney from Atlanta—I suppose he didn't want anyone here to know the gravity of the situation. He put what he had left into the startup of a cutting-edge technology firm. I'm sure he thought he'd make a complete financial recovery, had things gone well, but…" The attorney shrugged.

"But…" Faith moistened her lips. "But he said he was setting up a trust…"

"Yes. Well, I'm afraid he never got around to that, Mrs. Cameron."

She felt behind her for a chair and sank into it. She was numb.

"One asset, however, remains. The house. Mr. Cameron never touched it. It's free and clear."

The house. That big, drafty box where she'd never felt at home.

"It's a valuable property..."

Jergen kept talking. She heard the words "your inheritance" and "something of a surprise," but she wasn't really paying attention. The house was a valuable property. Those were the words echoing in her head, and suddenly she knew what to do. The chair squealed in protest as she pushed it back and got to her feet.

"Sell it," she said briskly. "Put the house on the market as soon as..."

Her words trickled to silence. Jergen's face had gone blank. And Cole—Cole was smiling. Warning bells rang in her head.

"What?" she said, looking from one man to the other. "Have I missed something? Mr. Jergen? Is there a reason I can't put the house on the market?"

"Mrs. Cameron." Jergen hesitated. "Mrs. Cameron," he said again and for the first time, she thought that he almost sounded human. "My dear young woman..."

"Never mind, Sam." Cole stepped past the lawyer. "I'll tell her."

"Tell me what?" Faith said uncertainly.

He smiled, reached out and touched her cheek with his hand. Despite the panic fluttering like crazed butterflies in her stomach, some small part of her registered the feel of his skin against hers and she caught her breath, stunned at how electrifying the sensation was.

"Don't!" She caught his wrist, jerked his hand away. "Tell me what?" she said again, and his smile tilted.

"You can't sell Cameron House, Faith."

"Why not? Is it because of probate? I thought the will had—"

"It has nothing to do with probate. I guess you weren't paying attention when old Sam, here, explained the facts of life." Cole's smile became an outright grin. "Stop counting those dollar signs, baby. Ted left the house to me."

* * *

Faith took a steadying breath as she pulled out of the parking lot and turned onto Main Street.

"Would you like some water?" Jergen had asked her, after Cole's incredible announcement.

"No," she'd replied, "no, I'm fine."

Fine enough to exchange a few more sentences and then walk from the conference room, through the office, out of the building and into the hot, hot sun that did nothing to stop the chill that crept through her as she began seeing just how precarious her situation was.

Ted had talked about setting up a trust for Peter, but he hadn't. He'd left his money to her, instead, but he'd lost it all. Nothing remained but Cameron House...and he'd willed that to Cole.

Her hands tightened on the steering wheel.

Whatever Ted had done with his money and his home was his affair. That was how she'd wanted it. All she'd ever let him give her was the Cameron name, and she'd done that for her son. Nobody could take away Peter's legitimacy. Not ever, but now she was a woman with a young son who'd have no roof over his head two days from now.

"When do you want me out of the house?" she'd asked Cole.

"Yesterday," he'd replied politely. "But I suppose the end of the month will have to do."

And she'd said, "Fine," as if it didn't matter.

What a stupid thing to have done. She'd been so busy trying not to let the terror of what was happening show that she'd been incapable of thinking straight. Everything was a mess and she'd only made things worse by being angry, not just at Cole for his smugness or Sam Jergen for the way he'd toadied up to him, but at Ted, too. Okay, that was wrong but, dammit, how could he have let this happen? If only he'd put the money in trust for Peter, instead of leaving it for her. If only he hadn't gone crazy in the stock market.

"If only pigs could fly," she whispered, and gave a laugh that sounded sad, even to her.

What was she going to tell Peter? The last couple of weeks,

they'd played a kind of game. She'd started it to put a smile on his face but the truth was, it had become as important to her as to him.

"When we move far, far away from here," she'd say, and Peter would counter with all the wishes in his child's heart.

When we move far, far away, I'm gonna live in a little house with a big yard instead of a big house on top of a hill. And I'm gonna have a puppy and a horse and a kitten.

All right. Maybe there wouldn't be a little house with a big yard. Maybe there wouldn't be a puppy and a horse and a kitten. But she and Peter would have each other. They'd live someplace where they'd just be a woman and a little boy, not that Davenport woman and the kid she'd used to get Ted Cameron's ring on her finger.

Except, how was she going to do that? She couldn't take off on a bus with a little boy and no destination, no money and no job. Job? Faith choked back something that was half sob, half laugh. You had to have skills to get a job and she had none, unless bandaging scraped knees counted as a talent.

Growing up, she'd picked peaches and beans and whatever crops were in season. At fifteen, she'd put on an apron and waitressed at the counter in the five-and-dime. She could do those things again, she wasn't afraid of hard work, but no matter what kind of job she got, what would she do about Peter? Who would take care of him? Summer was here. School was out, he'd be home and she'd sooner die than leave him on his own, here or anywhere.

The light ahead changed to red. Faith stepped too hard on the brake and the car jerked to a stop. She wanted to scream, to sob, to pound her fist against the steering wheel but that wouldn't change anything. Minutes ago, she'd been worried about how to tell Peter that the game of "When we move away from here" was ended. Now, she faced the realization that the game was the least of her problems.

"Reality time," Faith whispered, and pulled into the driveway that led to Cameron House—to Cole's house. She hit the button that opened the garage door and she pulled into the darkness, shut off the engine and let the door come down behind her.

A bone-deep weariness made her fold her arms over the steering wheel and lay her cheek against them. She didn't have time for self-pity. There had to be a way to get through this, even if it meant phoning Sam Jergen and asking him to convince Cole to let her stay on here for another week or two, just until she got things together.

Faith sat up straight, wiped her eyes and headed into the house. "Peter?" she called. There was no answer. All she could hear was the low hum of the air conditioner. "Peter? Where are you, honey?"

A note was tucked under a magnet on the refrigerator door. It was from Alice, the housekeeper. Alice despised her but she loved Peter. She'd taken him with her to the market.

Faith let out a breath. Good. She'd have time to get hold of herself...and go back to town and pick up the burger and fries she'd promised to buy. She did some quick calculating, amazed at what a dent four dollars and change would put into her budget, but she wasn't going to turn her son's life inside out if she could help it.

First, though, she'd get out of this straitjacket of a suit.

She went up the stairs to her bedroom, moving as slowly as if she'd aged a hundred years in the past couple of hours. The room was warm and she started to turn the thermostat down, thought of the possible cost of those few degrees and decided she could endure the heat.

Faith unzipped her skirt and tossed it on a chair. Her jacket followed. She reached for the top button on her blouse but it was already...

Cole had opened it.

An image flashed through her mind. She saw herself lying on the sofa in the law office, coming back to consciousness in his arms. For one breathless instant, time had seemed to run backward. She'd looked into his eyes and remembered awakening the same way the night they'd made love down by the lake, except then he'd smiled when she looked at him, whispered her name, taken her mouth in a hot, drugging kiss that had turned her boneless with desire...

What a fool she was!

Why was she giving in so easily? He'd always gotten what he wanted from her. Her innocence. Her love. Now, he was going to take this house but she belonged here more than he did. Cameron House had been her home for nine years. Cole hadn't been back in all that time. He'd left Liberty and never looked back, not at his brother, not at his father, not at her.

He wanted the house? Well, let him try and get it. So what if Ted had willed it to him? She was here and possession was nine-tenths of the law. She'd find a lawyer who'd be pleased to represent her, not somebody who'd bow down to a Cameron. What judge would force a woman and her child onto the streets?

Faith smiled. She could almost feel the load lifting from her heart.

Quickly, she flung off the rest of her clothes, shook out her hair and went into the bathroom. A cool shower would make her feel human again. She turned the spray to high and stepped under the water, letting it cascade over her face and body as if the force of it could wash away every last remnant of the awful morning.

She'd made things so easy. Cole was probably sitting in Jergen's office, laughing over how she'd crept away in defeat.

Well, he was in for a big surprise.

She dried off, pushed her wet hair back from her face and slipped on a short cotton robe. She was smiling as she walked into the bedroom. *Ready or not, Cole Cameron*, she thought, *here I...*

The brave idea ended on a shocked scream. Cole was standing in the doorway, his face twisted with rage, his hands knotted into fists at his sides.

"Faith," he growled. "Where is he?"

God, she thought, God, please help me...

"Where is he?" he said again and when she didn't answer, he kicked the door shut and came straight toward her.

All she could do was let out a strangled sob and fall back against the wall.

CHAPTER FOUR

COLE hadn't even thought about going to the house.

He'd watched Faith leave the law office, her chin lifted even though her face was ashen, her walk brisk.

"Tough spot to find herself in," Jergen had said, after a minute.

"Yeah." Cole had smiled thinly. "So is life."

"I don't feel sorry for the woman at all, you understand...but perhaps you should give her just a bit more time to vacate Cameron House."

Cole had looked at him as if he'd lost his mind. "What for?"

"Well, it's not very much notice, Mr. Cameron. If she went before a judge he'd probably grant her thirty days, maybe more."

"I'm not a judge. And if she has half the brains I figure, she'll know better than to waste the little money she has on legal fees."

"I agree, sir. I only meant, all things considered..."

"What things?" Cole looked at the lawyer and saw, to his surprise, that the man's face had suddenly become shiny with sweat. "Talk English, Jergen. I'm not in the mood for riddles."

"Perhaps I should have mentioned it sooner. I do have a certain obligation to maintain the privacy of my clients, but—"

"But?"

"But, it isn't as if there's only Mrs. Cameron in that house."

The conference room seemed to fill with silence.

"Isn't there?" Cole finally said, his voice low.

"No." The lawyer searched for the right words. "I mean, if she were alone, perhaps..."

"Get to it, man. Who's living at that house with my sister-in-law?"

Jergen inhaled sharply, then blew the breath out through pursed lips. "Peter. And, of course, she won't have the money to support—"

Cole's blood drummed in his ears, drowning out whatever else the attorney was saying. The room swam, then went crimson. He shouldered his way past Jergen, ran down the stairs but Faith was gone. And a good thing, he thought as he dumped his jacket in the back seat, got behind the wheel of the Jaguar and gunned the powerful engine to life.

His brother was hardly cold in his grave and his wife had taken herself a lover and installed him under the Cameron roof, supported him with Cameron money...

Cole stepped down on the gas. Horns blared as he threaded his way through traffic, skidded around street corners and headed instinctively for the back roads he'd once ridden on his motorcycle whenever he'd needed to clear his head.

The houses began thinning. The air he pulled into his lungs no longer held the stench of the town. Open fields and woods flashed by. At last, the road turned to dirt and arrowed toward the hills and infinity.

Cole jammed his foot to the floor. The car gave a throaty roar and leaped ahead but the knot inside him only tightened. He'd seen what he'd come for, the look on Faith's face when she'd learned her scheme had fallen through, but it wasn't enough anymore. Not after what Jergen had told him.

His sweet sister-in-law had a man. A lover, living with her in that damnable house, sleeping in her bed, kissing and caressing that body she'd once offered him.

"Hell," Cole said roughly, and the tires screamed as he stood on the brakes and put the Jaguar into a tight turn that left a rooster tail of hot Georgia dust rising behind him. He needed to see it for himself.

Twenty minutes later, Cameron House had loomed against the sky as big and ugly as he'd remembered. There was no car in the driveway, no sign of life, but he hadn't expected any. Faith would have put her car in the garage. By now, she was probably in her lover's arms, telling him the money they'd been counting on was gone.

Only a rich widow could afford to take herself a stud and pay for his services.

He took the front steps two at a time, strode across a porch that bore testament to his old man's inability to know the difference between schlock and style, and stabbed the doorbell until his finger hurt. Then he pounded his fist against the door.

"Faith," he said. His voice rose to a roar. "Faith!"

Nothing. The door remained shut, the house stayed silent. Cole ground his teeth together. He'd be damned if he'd stand out here, cooling his heels while his beloved sister-in-law sought the comfort of her lover's arms.

He eyed the door. He could use his shoulder to batter it open... Hell, he didn't have to. In his rage, he'd almost forgotten the brass key that had always been tucked under the doormat. Was it still...? Yes. It was. He dug it out, shoved it into the lock and the door swung open.

Nothing had changed. The foyer was still dark and gloomy, the furniture still overstuffed, oversized and overbearing.

Cole could feel the adrenaline pumping through his body. The metallic taste of his rage was in his mouth, the power of it in his muscles. He could almost smell it rising from his skin.

"Faith?"

He moved through the rooms quickly, knowing as he did that he wouldn't find her down here, that she'd be upstairs...that he could be walking into something he didn't want to see, but this was his house now, not hers, and he had every right to toss whoever was living with her out on his ass. She owed his brother's memory some respect. That was the only reason for his anger, for the way his blood was driving through his veins.

"Faith?" he'd shouted, and started up the stairs. That was when he'd heard the hiss of water. Someone was taking a shower.

He'd flung open the door to the master bedroom. Empty.

He'd marched down the hall to the room that had been Ted's. Empty.

"Faith, you…"

He'd spun in a tight circle, cocked his head…and realized the sound was coming from the room that had once been his. Frowning, he'd walked slowly to the door, put his hand on the knob and turned it. To his surprise, the room was almost exactly as he'd left it. The same furniture, the same curtains and spread. The scent in the air was all that was different.

Faith's scent.

And, just then, the bathroom door had opened and she'd stepped into the bedroom, Faith, wearing a thin cotton robe that clearly outlined her breasts; Faith, her hair damp and wild and streaming down her back; Faith, her long legs bare and elegant as they'd been when they'd closed around his waist that long ago night.

The knot in Cole's belly had tightened until it threatened to rise into his throat.

"Faith," he said, and she turned, saw him and screamed.

The scream, the heart-stopping terror in her beautiful face, only fed his rage. "Where is he?" he said, and she went even whiter. She staggered back against the wall as he kicked the door shut.

"I asked you a question. Where is he?"

"Who?"

"You know damned well, who." Cole pushed her aside, looked into the bathroom. Steam curled lazily from its empty depths. "Peter, that's who." He moved past her again, yanked open the closet door even though he couldn't imagine anybody was hiding inside. Faith hadn't heard him coming; neither would her lover, but he was operating on instinct now, the primitive part of his brain taking over despite the layers of civility and centuries of evolution that were supposed to have tamed it. Furious, his blood still drumming in his ears, he swung around and glared at her. "Tell me where he is."

He knew. Oh, he knew! Faith reached behind her, put her hand on the nightstand for support. It was inevitable that he'd learn about Peter's existence, but she hadn't expected such rage...

"Answer me, dammit. Where is he?"

"How did you...?" Her voice shook. "I don't know."

Cole's eyes swept over her. She flushed, fought against the almost overwhelming urge to grab the cover from the bed and wrap herself in it, but the last thing she wanted was to let him know how vulnerable she felt. Alice, she thought desperately, Alice, wherever you are, don't come home just yet.

"Come on, baby. You can do better than that. He's here, all right. What man in his right mind wouldn't be waiting to see you come out of that shower?"

"I'm telling you, I don't..." Faith caught her breath. *Man?*

"Don't tell me he's gone already." Cole's mouth twisted. "Did you tell him about the money? Does he know you won't be able to support yourself on what little is left, let alone support a lover?"

Cole didn't know she had a son, he thought she had a lover. A lover! The idea was preposterous and so far removed from what she'd thought he believed that she almost laughed. In fact—in fact...

The sound rose in her throat and burst from her mouth. Cole's face turned red and she clamped her lips together. Don't, she told herself, don't, but it was too late. She shook with hysterical laughter, with the relief of it, the pain of it...

Cole's hands bit into her shoulders. "Who are you laughing at, my brother or me?"

"I'm—not—laughing," she gasped, but she was, she was laughing and weeping and—

"Damn you," Cole growled, and hauled her into his arms and kissed her.

It all happened so fast that, later, he cursed himself for a fool. He hadn't been thinking, hadn't been functioning or he'd never have done it. Why would he kiss her? She was all the things he most despised in a woman, a scheming little liar with an uncanny talent for taking a perfectly normal male and making him do things he'd never have dreamed of doing.

None of that reasoning drove him now. Anger drove him,

a fury so hot and deep and dark that he didn't give a damn that she was struggling frantically to free herself of his embrace or that she was trying to twist her mouth away from his. She owed him this, owed him for the years of hating her and wanting her and asking himself when he was ever going to purge her from his system.

"Stop," she begged, and he laughed, thrust a hand into her hair, tilted her head back and kissed her again and again, his mouth hard, his hands rough...and then she made a sound that cut through it all, a whisper of fear and despair, and it pierced what little remained of his heart.

"Faith," he whispered, and his kiss softened, became a plea. His mouth moved gently over hers. He said her name again, put both hands in her hair, and she sighed and opened her mouth to his.

A thousand memories swept through him. The warm, silken softness of her skin under his caressing hands. The honeyed sweetness of her mouth, the flower-and-rain scent of her hair. The feel of her against him, her breasts thrusting against his chest, her hips tilted up just enough so he could press his aroused flesh into the vee of her thighs when he swept one hand down her back, cupped her bottom, lifted her to him.

She was the woman he had never forgotten, a dizzying blend of sensuality and innocence. Having her in his arms again, feeling her surrender, sent all his blood to his loins.

He groaned and buried his face at the tender juncture of neck and shoulder. He'd always loved the smell and taste of her there. All he'd ever had to do was kiss that spot, catch the skin lightly between his teeth and she'd moan, her head would fall back and his name would whisper from her lips...

As it did now. Her hands had been pressed against his chest. Now, they curled into his shirt. He felt her shudder and he knew she was trying to deny what she felt but it was too late. He slid his hands inside her robe and cupped her breasts. God, the feel of her. The heat. He moved his thumbs over her nipples and she cried out his name.

"Cole. Cole, please..."

The words took him back in time, made him hard as stone—and made him remember what a talented Jezebel she was.

He let go of her. Faith staggered back, opened her eyes and stared at him. If he hadn't known better, he'd have thought the horror on her face was real.

"God," he said hoarsely. He swung away from her and gulped deep lungfuls of air. He felt sick to his stomach. It disgusted him, to think she could still affect him like this.

"You—you bastard!"

The blow to his back caught him by surprise. She struck him again and he turned, grabbed for her hands and pinned them against his chest but not before her fingernail raked his lip. Her eyes were bright with tears, her mouth trembled. She tried to jerk free of his grasp and bring up her knee, but he pushed her away and she fell backward onto the bed and looked up at him as if he were a monster.

"Get out of my house!"

Such righteous indignation. If he'd been a spectator instead of a participant in this pathetic excuse for a morality play, he'd have been tempted to believe she was the innocent virgin wronged by the evil villain. Cole took out his handkerchief, gingerly put it to his lip. The white linen came away faintly smeared with blood.

"Are you deaf?" Faith scooted across the bed and got to her feet. "Get out!"

"You're repeating yourself," he said coldly.

"And you're still here!"

"Maybe you had difficulty understanding what Sam Jergen said, Faith." He stuffed the handkerchief into his pocket. She was good, no doubt about it. She didn't only look wronged, she looked terrified. "This house is mine. Think about it, baby. You can't throw a man off his own property."

"The house is mine." She held the robe closer, lifted her chin, looked him in the eye. "I live here. I *have* lived her for the past nine years."

"And? You think that gives you squatter's rights?" Cole folded his arms over his chest. "My brother wrote a will. He left this place to me. End of story."

"Your brother was my husband. He said he'd leave me money only there wasn't any money to leave. I live here. You don't. Possession is nine-tenths of the law. *That's* the end of the story!"

"Is that what your lover told you?"

Color striped her face. "I don't need anyone to tell me right from wrong."

"Wednesday," Cole said coolly. "Nine a.m. You're either gone or—"

"Or what? You'll get the sheriff to evict *me?*" She flashed him a chilly smile and took the telephone from the nightstand. "How about I get him to evict *you?*"

"Nobody can evict me. I just told you, this house is—"

"Yours. And maybe it will be, when I'm good and ready to leave. Until then, I'm the one living here. That makes you an intruder." Her eyebrows lifted. "Last chance, Cole. Are you leaving on your own, or do you want to wait for the sheriff? I'm sure he'll be happy to do his civic duty and arrest you for trespass or breaking and entering. Whatever it's called."

"Go right ahead." Cole spoke with exaggerated politeness. "Call the sheriff, by all means. I'm certain he'll be eager to assist you."

He wouldn't. Cole knew it. So did she. The sheriff didn't think any better of her than anybody else in this miserable town. Still, facts were facts. He'd see what had happened, that Cole had broken into the house, that he looked as dangerous and disreputable as when he'd left Liberty nine years ago...

Faith caught her bottom lip between her teeth. Dangerous, yes. But not disreputable. What he looked was gorgeous and exciting, every woman's bad-boy fantasy come true.

Even hers.

That was the worst of it, that he'd taken her in his arms and tapped into all those hot, humiliating dreams she'd had as a girl. There were still times she came awake in the dark of night, her body aching for his remembered touch. She dreamed of his hands on her skin, his roughened fingers moving with shocking tenderness over her breasts, between her thighs.

Every memory of that one night they'd spent together was a part of her. The hardness of Cole's body. The sweetness of his mouth. The heat in his eyes and the excitement of knowing she'd caused it...

Faith turned her back to Cole and fumbled with the phone. Her brain wasn't functioning right. What was the sheriff's number? She couldn't remember and that was his fault, too, because he'd frightened her, angered her, made her remember things she'd spent years trying to forget.

How? How could he have done that? Made her want to melt against him, let him do the things he'd done to her throughout that incredible night?

"What's the matter, Faith?"

She jerked her chin up. He was watching her with an intensity that made the hair rise on the nape of her neck, as if he knew what she was thinking. Dammit, what was that number? She knew it. Everybody in town knew it. Six three one. No. Six four one. One four six...

"Hang up the phone." His voice was soft, almost a purr.

Faith turned her back. She didn't want to feel his eyes on her. The number, dammit. The number...

"I said, hang up."

His hands clasped her waist. She gasped and swung toward him. "Don't you dare touch me!"

"Why not?" His mouth turned up at the corners in a slow, sexy smile. "You know," he said softly, "I thought you were putting on a show a little while ago. Maybe I was wrong. Maybe the problem's more complicated than that."

"There'll be a very complicated problem for you, once I call the sheriff."

"I turn you on."

She blinked. His tone was filled with certainty and she wanted to laugh again—except it would be dangerous because he might take her in his arms again, if she laughed, he might kiss her...

She smiled. That was safe enough. "I'm amazed there's room in here for you, me—and your ego."

"It's true, isn't it?" He moved closer. She tried to move

back but the nightstand was right behind her. "You like sex. You always did."

His voice was thick and rough; his eyes were darkening. Faith could feel her heart beginning to race. She lifted the telephone, held it between them and punched the buttons. "I'm calling the sheriff."

"Sure. But you might want to think about what you'll tell him."

"I'll tell him the truth. That you broke into my house."

"Sheriff's Department," a tinny voice said in her ear.

"Really." Cole grinned, reached into his pocket, took out a key and held it in front of her. It was a duplicate of the old-fashioned brass key she owned. "Seems to me it's kind of difficult to accuse a man of breaking in when he used a key."

"Sheriff's Department," the voice said again. "Miss? Do you need help?"

Yes, Faith thought, but not the kind she'd find behind a sheriff's badge.

"No," she said, and took a breath. "Sorry. I—I must have dialed by mistake." Slowly, she put the telephone down. "All right. You've made your point. This is your house and I don't belong here."

"Damn right, you don't. You never did, and you sure as hell don't belong here with your latest—"

The door flew open. They both swung toward it. Faith felt her knees buckle. No, she thought, please, no...

"Mommy?" Peter bounced into the room. "Look what Alice got me... Oh." Her son stared past her. "Who's that?" he said, with childish directness.

Faith forced her lips to curve into what she hoped was a smile. "Peter," she said, "Peter, darling. Come and say hello to—to your uncle."

CHAPTER FIVE

FAITH had feared this moment, feared it for months after her baby's birth. But as time passed and months became years, life had been peaceful. It had lulled her into forgetfulness. Then she'd walked into Sam Jergen's office and the fear had come rushing back, filling her with terror.

Justifiable terror.

She'd known she had little hope of keeping Peter's existence a secret, not with Cole back in town. Sooner or later, somebody would say something. And somebody had. Someone—Jergen, probably, told him she had someone named Peter in her life. Cole thought he was her lover.

If only fate had left things that way...

But it hadn't.

Cole and his son were staring at each other, both of them looking as stunned as she felt, though for very different reasons. Their expressions were almost identical. Two pairs of wide green eyes. Two slightly dimpled chins. Two mouths, opened in surprise. Peter, a miniature of Cole. A miniature of his father...

No. No. Faith took a ragged breath. She must not think that way. Ted was Peter's father. Cole was from a time long past and best forgotten.

Peter recovered first. "Mom?" He looked at her. "Is he really my uncle?"

Faith gave a laugh so false she half expected a bolt of lightning to sizzle from the sky and strike her.

"Yes," she said brightly, "that's right, sweetheart. Your—your uncle."

Her son looked as if he couldn't decide if that was good news or bad. Faith swallowed hard. Cole, older and more capable of disguising his feelings, had masked his expression but he didn't take his eyes off Peter. What was he thinking? What did he see?

Not the truth. Oh, please, please, not the truth. "He looks just like Cole," Ted had said on Peter's first birthday. She'd denied it. He looks like himself, she'd insisted…but now she knew she'd been lying.

"How come you never said I had an uncle?"

Faith cleared her throat. "Well, I guess I didn't—I mean, I never thought…"

"No." Cole's voice was frigid. "I guess you never did."

Her heart thumped as he brushed past her. For one terrible, hope-filled instant, she thought he was going to ignore her son, march straight past him and out the door. No such luck. Cole stopped in front of the boy.

"Hello."

Peter shot a delighted look at her, then at Cole. "Hi," he said shyly.

Cole didn't answer. After what seemed forever, he bent down to Peter's level and held out his hand. "I'm Cole."

Her son hesitated. Then he held out his hand, too, and let Cole's swallow it up.

"How old are you, Pete?"

Faith realized she'd been holding her breath and let it out in one long rush. "It's Peter," she said quickly. Two sets of green eyes fixed on her, one bright with childish wonder, the other icy with tightly banked rage. "His name is—"

"It's Peter," her little boy said. "But—but some of the guys call me Pete."

The sweet lie almost broke Faith's heart. There were no "guys" and no nicknames. Her son smiled hopefully at Cole, who smiled back.

"Pete it is, then. How old are you, Pete?"

No, Faith thought. She wanted to grab her son and run but there was no place to run to.

"I'm eight."

"Eight." Cole nodded, let go of the kid's hand and told himself to take it easy. It all made sense now. He'd misunderstood Sam Jergen; he'd assumed Faith had only claimed to be pregnant but she really had been. Ted could never have walked away from his own son. He'd have done the right thing.

"Eight," Cole he repeated, his voice soft as silk, his anger as deadly as one of the superheated fires that could turn an oil well into a never-ending spiral of flame.

"Yup. How old are you?"

He took a deep breath, reminded himself that the child's genes were only half Davenport. Cameron blood ran through the boy's veins, too. Ted's blood.

"I'm just a few years older than that," he said, smiling as best he could around his fury. While he'd still been aching for Faith, she'd been carrying his brother's child.

"How come I never knew nothing about you?"

"Anything," Faith said. It was as inane as her first comment but she couldn't just stand here in silence. She had to end this meeting before it dragged on any longer. Man and child looked at her again and she ran the tip of her tongue between her lips. "I mean—I mean surprises are nice sometimes, Peter, don't you think?"

Cole rose slowly to his feet. "Good question, Faith. Why not ask it of me?"

"Cole." She took a breath. "Look, I'm sure you have—you have questions, but—"

"Me? Questions?" His mouth twisted. "Not a one, baby. Why would I have questions when any man with half a brain can figure out the answers?" His eyes swept over her, all but peeling the robe from her body. "I told Ted to take care of you," he said softly. "I should have told him to take care of himself."

"You told him to take care of me?" Faith gave a quick, bitter laugh. "Please. Let's not lie to each other, not after all these years. I was the last thing you thought of, after that night—"

"What night?"

Faith caught her breath. Peter was looking up at her, his head cocked to the side. She bent down, lifted him up even though he was really too big for that, and hugged him.

"Hey," she said briskly, "you know what?"

"Put me down, Mommy." Peter shot an embarrassed look over her shoulder. "I'm not a baby anymore."

"I will, in a minute. Give me a hug first. That's it." She put her son on his feet, smiled and ruffled his hair. "I just remembered that I didn't get you that burger I promised. Why don't I take you to town—"

"You might want to get dressed first," Cole said softly.

Her eyes flashed to his face. He was smiling thinly and she told herself not to blush, not to give him the pleasure of seeing her discomfort.

"I'll put on some jeans and a T-shirt," she said, her voice gentle for Peter, her eyes icy for Cole. "And we'll drive to town—"

"I already had a hamburger. Alice bought me one."

"Oh." Faith nodded. "Well, then—then we'll go to—to the Ice Cream Factory for—"

"Mom," her sweet, adorable, faithless little boy said, "it's too near suppertime for ice cream. That's what you always say."

"Is it?" Faith glanced at the clock on the nightstand. He was right. A lifetime had passed since this morning. How could that be? "Well…" Well, what? Cole wasn't showing any signs of leaving. He was standing with his hands in his pockets, his eyes locked on her face. "Well, since it's that late, we'll drive into town anyway and—and pick up some fried chicken. And—and a video. We'll have an early supper in the den. On trays." She knew she probably sounded desperate, and she was. There had to be a way to get away from Cole and that unreadable stare.

Peter looked at her. "That sounds like fun," he said politely. Then he beamed a smile at Cole. "You know somethin'? I didn't have an uncle when I woke up this morning."

Cole gave her son a smile. "Well, I didn't have a nephew, so I guess we're even."

"Are you my mommy's brother or my daddy's? That's what uncles are, right? Brothers?"

"Peter," Faith said quickly, "why don't you go get cleaned up so we can—"

"That's what they are, Pete. I'm your father's brother."

"Oh." Peter's face turned solemn. "My father is dead. Did you know that?"

"Yeah." Cole's mouth thinned into a hard line. "Yeah, I knew."

"So, is that why you came here? 'Cause my father's dead and now you're gonna take care of Mommy and me?"

"Peter!" Faith knew she'd spoken harshly. The man and the boy looked at her, her son with surprise and Cole with something so feral glittering in his eyes that it made her breath catch, but she didn't care. This couldn't go on. It absolutely could not continue. "Peter, you know it's not polite to ask so many questions."

"Not of a stranger, maybe." Cole's tone was cutting. "But I'm hardly that, Faith. I'm his blood, even if you'd have preferred to keep me from knowing it."

"Please." She shot him an imploring look. "Let's not discuss this now."

"No. Let's not." A muscle knotted in his jaw. "But I promise you, we're going to discuss it later."

"Discuss what?" Peter said. "If you're going to stay here and—"

"Peter," Faith said, and forced a smile, "don't you want us to go get that video?"

"Sure," he said, but he was looking up at Cole. "Am I supposed to call you Cole? Or Uncle Cole?"

"Cole will do just fine."

"Well," Faith said briskly, "isn't it nice that you two met? Cole, we don't want to keep you. I know you were on your way out the door when—"

"Yes," Cole said in a deceptively lazy drawl, "that's right. Strangely enough, I was just on my way into town to see if that old fried chicken place is still down on Main Street. I guess it is, considering your plans for the evening."

"Yes. It is. But—"

"Isn't that the craziest coincidence? I figured I'd pick some up, bring it back here and we'd all have an early dinner. How's that sound, Pete?''

"No," Faith blurted. "I mean, thank you but we couldn't possibly impose."

"It's no imposition." His eyes fixed on hers, that cold flame still burning in their depths. "After all, Faith, we're family."

"We're fam'ly, Mommy."

The innocent accuracy of the words made Faith want to scream. "I'd love to say yes," she lied, "but—but. It's too early for dinner…"

"You just said it wasn't," Peter said, his lower lip pushing out a little.

"Come on, Faith." Cole spoke softly. "Try, just once, not to let things go until it's too late."

She stared at him, knowing the trap was closing around her and there was nothing she could do to stop it.

"It's just…" She stopped, started again. "It's just fried chicken. And a video from the children's section. You'll be—you'll be bored."

Cole smiled. Once again, his gaze stripped her naked. "Nothing about you could ever bore a man."

She felt her cheeks redden. "Fine," she said, the word as clipped and cold as she could make it. "Do what you like. Go to town, buy the chicken, rent a video. If you insist on spending the evening here, there's nothing I can do to stop you short of bolting the door—" She caught herself, forced a smile. "Peter and I will be waiting."

"You'll be waiting." Cole put his hand on Peter's shoulder. "Pete and I are going to town."

"No!"

"You'll have to show me where the video store is," Cole said, ignoring her completely. "There wasn't any, when I lived here."

"It's right near the chicken place," Peter said, nearly jumping up and down with excitement. "What we do is, we order the chicken and then—"

"Are you both deaf? I said no."

Again, their faces turned to her but this time instead of

panic, what she felt was anger. How dare Cole Cameron come stomping back into her life and take over? She wasn't about to let that happen and the sooner he knew it, the better.

"My son is staying with me." Faith stepped forward, put her hands on Peter's shoulders and drew him away from Cole. "I've no intention of letting him go anywhere with you. Do you think I'm crazy? My boy is not—" Is not going to grow up to be like you, she almost said, caught herself just in time and, instead, spoke the first words that came into her head. "My boy is not going to ride on the back of a motorcycle."

"Oh, wow. A motorcycle?" Her son was almost breathless with awe. "Have you got a motorcycle? Where? I didn't see it outside. I just saw that long black car. It's got a cat's picture on it."

Cole laughed. "You're an observant kid, you know that?" He looked at Faith. "It's a Jaguar," he said. "Brand new, with all possible safety bells and whistles. Destroys a whole bucket of illusions, doesn't it?"

Trapped, she thought again, trapped.

"Mommy? Can I go with Cole? Say yes, Mommy, please."

Every instinct told her to say no, to tell Cole that this house still belonged to her and she wanted him out of it, right now. But he wouldn't leave any more than he'd accept her answer. And then there was Peter. His face was lit with excitement. For the first time in weeks, he looked happy.

"All right," she said, accepting defeat. "You can go." She reached for her son and hugged him again. "I love you," she whispered.

"Me, too," Peter said, but with the eager impatience of a child about to set off on a great adventure. He wiggled free of her arms and grinned at Cole. "We can get the stuff and Mommy can get dressed while we're gone."

Cole took his time looking her over, from the top of her head to her toes. She knew her face was burning.

"Out of the mouths of babes," he said politely, and their eyes met. "You know, Faith, it only just occurred to me... Did you suspect I was going to pay a visit? Did Jergen phone, perhaps, and suggest I might be stopping by?" His smile froze. "And did you dress accordingly?"

"What's 'accordingly'?" Peter asked.

"It's a grown-up word," Cole said. "It means when someone does something deliberately."

"That's not what it means at all," Faith said tightly.

Cole smiled. Then he turned the smile on Peter. She saw it become real and warm. He held out his hand. Peter took it. And the child she loved and the man she hated strolled casually out the door.

The trip to town and back should have taken half an hour. Forty-five minutes, if the chicken wasn't ready for pickup and Peter dawdled the way he almost always did when he chose a video.

At the two hour point, Faith was almost frantic. Where was her son? Where was Cole? And why had she let him intimidate her? He was every cliché in the book, the proverbial bad penny that always turned up, still looking as dangerous and unsettled as he had at eighteen, and never mind the Jaguar. She wasn't an impressionable teenaged girl anymore.

Cole had come back only to lay claim to Ted's estate. He'd discovered she had a son and laid claim to him, too. And what had she done? She'd let him get away with it, just as he had years before.

What Cole wanted, Cole got. For whatever reason, he wanted to impress Peter. And she'd let him, dammit, let him maneuver her into compliance while he won her son's smiles with an offer of greasy fried chicken and a stupid video and a ride in a car he'd probably gone into hock to rent...

The phone rang. Faith grabbed for it. "Where the hell are you?" she demanded.

Cole laughed. "So much for hospitality."

"So much for responsibility. Do you have any idea how long you've been gone?"

"A little longer than we planned, I guess."

"You guess?" She heard the hysteria in her voice, took a

deep breath and started again. "I asked you a question. Where are you?"

"Where are we, Pete?" Cole said.

Pete, she thought, with what the still-functioning part of her brain told her was senseless rage, Pete! She couldn't make out her son's response but she could hear his childish excitement. And over what? Over a pathetic bit of attention from the man who'd planted him in her womb and never looked back?

"Cole."

"Yeah, I heard you. Pete says—"

"His name is Peter."

"Yeah, so you told me. We're on North Road, maybe two miles from—"

"I know where North Road is."

"Well, I didn't. It's new. Pete took me on a little tour. The town's changed since I last saw it."

"The town isn't all that's changed. You can't walk all over me anymore." She fought to get herself under control. "Bring my son home immediately."

Faith banged down the phone. Things had changed in Liberty and so had she.

When the doorbell rang half an hour later, she was ready for him. She thought she was, anyway, but she wasn't ready for the sight of her little boy, hanging on to Cole's hand, looking not just happy but worshipful. Looking every inch his father's son.

"Peter," she said, "go to your room."

"But the chicken's hot—"

"Go to your room, Peter."

Her son's lip trembled. "We got *Aladdin*," he said. "Right, Cole? 'Cause Cole said he never saw it..."

"You can watch it later," Faith said, her eyes on Cole's face.

"Cole said he read the book, when he was a kid like me. Cole said—"

"I don't give a da..." Faith took a couple of quick, deep breaths. "Peter. If you want to see that video, go to your room now. Otherwise, you'll get a time out."

Tears welled in the child's eyes. "That's not fair. You said—"

"Hey." Cole squatted down, put his hands on the boy's shoulders and smiled. "Your mom's upset, Petey."

Petey, Faith thought crazily. Petey. He was explaining her to her own son, a child who'd gone from being Peter to Pete to Petey in the blink of an eye.

"She's upset with me, not with you." He stood up, still smiling, but his eyes were chips of winter ice. "Isn't that right, Faith?"

"Yes," she said, hating herself for not making it clear to Peter that her temper had nothing to do with him, hating Cole even more for having the presence of mind to have done it for her. "Yes," she said gently. "That's right. This has nothing to do with you, sweetheart."

"Okay." Peter rubbed the back of his hand over his eyes. "So can we—"

"No." Her voice was sharp; she tried to temper it with a smile. "Cole and I have to talk. Grown-up stuff, Peter. It would only bore you." Faith put her hand on her son's head. "Tell you what. You leave everything right here, Cole and I will—we'll have our chat and—and in a little while, you can come down and we'll watch the movie together."

"All three of us?"

"Peter." Faith took a breath. "Do as you're told."

The boy looked at Cole. "Go on, champ," Cole said softly. "I'll see you later."

"Promise?"

"Yeah. I promise."

The child hesitated. Then he stepped forward and threw his arms around the man he thought was his uncle. Because of the differences in their height, the boy enfolded Cole's legs. It caught Cole by surprise; what was even more of a surprise was that the simple action made his throat constrict.

He'd never noticed kids very much; they were everywhere you looked but not part of his world. It amazed him that this little boy should have gotten under his skin so quickly but then, this was Ted's flesh and blood. This was his nephew...

And if he'd stayed in Liberty, if he hadn't had to run away to protect Faith's reputation, this might have been his son. If he'd stayed, if he'd told Faith he wanted to marry her, if she'd said that she would...

"Everything will be fine," he said briskly. "Now, go on. The sooner your mother and I have our talk, the sooner we can dig into that chicken."

Peter stepped back. "You mean it?"

"Give me a break, champ. Would I pass up the chance to fight you over who gets the supercrispy wings?"

Peter laughed. Then he whirled around and ran up the stairs. Faith watched him go. When she heard the sound of his bedroom door close, she looked at Cole.

"In the library," she said coolly, and set off down the hall.

Cole raised his brows. "Yes, ma'am," he drawled and followed her into the dark-paneled room. The door swung shut after him.

The room hadn't changed at all. There were still the same ugly damask draperies, the same mud-brown leather furniture. Faith chose a ladder-backed chair. Cole settled on the sofa, stretched out his long legs and folded his arms behind his head. He'd rolled up his shirtsleeves and she tried not to notice how the casual posture emphasized the swell of muscle in his biceps.

"You shouldn't have done that," she said.

"Done what?" His tone was innocence personified. "Even my old man let me sit on the sofa in here, Faith. Or are you telling me to sit up straight, keep my feet together and my hands in my lap, the way he'd have done?" He grinned. "If you are, you're in for a disappointment."

"You know what I mean. Telling those lies to Peter—"

"I'm not a liar."

"Of course you are. You lied to me years ago. Now you're lying to my son."

"What happened between you and me has nothing to do with this. I'd never lie to the kid."

Faith shot to her feet. "What else would you call those promises you made him? That you're going to be here when he comes downstairs again? That you're going to have supper here, and watch some—some dumb kid's movie with him..."

She stared at him, shocked by her anger. There was nothing dumb about kids' movies, especially when you were curled on the couch with a child, sharing his excitement and laughter. *She* was what was dumb, otherwise she wouldn't be looking at this man she hated and thinking how handsome he was. She wouldn't be remembering that when he'd worn white shirts like this, with the collar open and the sleeves rolled back, it had made her as hot as the weather just to look at him. She wouldn't remember how she'd loved to slide her hands beneath the shirt, spread her palms over his muscled chest, feel the heat of his skin...

"Just—just get out," she whispered. "Go away before you do any real damage, Cole. Before you make any more promises you have no intention of keeping."

He rose to his feet, his face stony. "I told you, this has nothing to do with us."

"Yes, it does. It has everything to do with us. I know you. I know what you're really like, under all that—that charm." Her throat tightened. She swallowed, then began again. "But Peter is just a little boy. He's at an age where he believes whatever people tell him. Can you understand that?"

"You're the one who needs to understand, Faith." Slowly, he started toward her, his eyes never leaving her face. "I didn't lie to the kid."

"You said you'd be here for supper."

"I will be."

"And that you'd watch a movie with him."

"I'll do that, too."

"Cole, be reasonable. Even if I let you stay this evening—"

"If you *let* me?" Darkness clouded his face. "You seem to forget, baby. This is my house. If I want to stay here for supper, hell, if I want to stay here until the next century, I can do it."

"You can't. No court—"

"Ah." Cole tucked his hands into the pockets of his trousers and rocked back on his heels. "So, that's what this is all about. You figure sharing this roof with me, even for a few hours, might put you in legal limbo.''

"No, of course not. I never thought—"

"That's right. You never thought. Not once." His mouth twisted. He jerked his hands from his pockets, reached out and clamped his fingers around her arms. "Not when you were seducing my brother, not when you were getting yourself knocked up—"

Faith yanked her arms free. "Get out. Get out of my house!" Her voice trembled; every part of her trembled as she raised a hand and pointed it at him. "Get—out!"

They stared at each other, the silence broken only by the sound of Faith's rapid breathing and the steady tick of the clock on the mantel over the fireplace.

"Listen to me," Cole said softly, "and listen well, baby. This house is mine."

"It isn't. I live here and—"

"You live here. I own it. Maybe, if you concentrate hard enough, you'll start to see the difference."

"Cole." Faith wrapped her arms around herself. Despite the late afternoon heat, she felt cold straight into the marrow of her bones. "Cole, I—I—"

"You what? You're going to get yourself a lawyer and fight me? What will you pay your legal fees with, huh?"

"That's just the…" Her breath shuddered. "That's the point. I have no money. And—and I know you don't give a damn how that affects me—"

"You're right, I don't."

"But there's—there's my son."

"Ted's son, you mean."

"Yes. Ted's—Ted's son." She looked up, her eyes filled with pleading. "Peter's just a little boy. He has no part in any of this."

Cole folded his arms over his chest. "Go on."

She had to go on. She had no choice. Cole held the winning hand. What did pride matter now?

"It's not as if I want to stay in this house."

He smiled thinly. "Good. Because you're not going to."

"I'd already made plans to leave Liberty. To start over again, someplace where nobody knows us."

"Right. Someplace where you can find another sucker who won't have the disadvantage of knowing you kept my brother out of your bed."

"You don't know anything about my relationship with Ted."

"Don't I?"

He moved toward her. Faith saw the look in his face and moved back.

"No. You don't. I—I loved Ted."

"You don't know the meaning of the word."

"I loved him. And we both loved Peter. And—"

"Keep the boy out of this!"

"I can't do that. Peter's the reason I want to move away. I just need some time to—to get my life together. Find a job, in Atlanta."

Cole laughed. "Women with your skills don't find jobs, Faith, they find fools to support them."

"Find a job," she said, her face coloring, her chin lifting, her eyes steady on his. "I can commute. I can save money. Then I can move away."

"You can do that now. Move away, I mean."

"I just told you, I can't. I need money…"

She gasped as Cole caught hold of her and pulled her against him. "What you need," he said roughly, "is a man."

"No. No—"

His mouth crushed hers in a kiss filled with anger and passion too long denied. Faith cried out, tried to twist away and he imprisoned her hands between his while his mouth slanted over hers. He thrust his tongue between her lips, tasting what he had never forgotten, and all at once the years rolled away. He was eighteen again, she was his girl. And she was in his arms, kissing him back…

Kissing him back, as she was now, with her hands in his hair, her body lifted to fit against his. With her little cries, her very breath shared between them. She was his, she was all he'd ever wanted…

God!

Cole thrust her from him and wiped the back of his hand across his mouth. He saw her eyes open, saw the confusion in their depths and for one wild instant he almost believed she was as stunned by the power of that hungry kiss as he was.

He took a couple of breaths and regained his sanity.

"It won't work," he said in a low voice. "I know what you are. I'm not a kid anymore, Faith. And I'm sure as hell not my brother."

"No." Her voice quivered. She gave a little laugh and blinked back her tears. "You aren't."

"Tell the boy I'm sorry but I had to leave."

"Of course."

"Tell him I didn't mean to make a promise and then break it."

"No." The words were tinged with irony. "Certainly not."

Cole walked to the door. He started to open it, then turned and looked at her. "What time does he go to bed?"

"Nine. But I don't see—"

"Tell him he can stay up later than usual tonight." He looked at his watch, then at her. "If he can hold out that long, we'll have supper in two hours and watch that video."

"What are you talking about? I thought we'd agreed—"

"Haven't you figured it out yet, baby? I'm the guy making the rules. You don't get to 'agree' to anything."

Cole stepped into the hall. She ran after him, calling his name, demanding he come back and explain what he'd said...

And ended up standing on the porch, watching the dust raised by the Jaguar as he gunned the engine and shot out of the driveway.

CHAPTER SIX

COLE had always driven fast. Too fast, sometimes, especially when he was a kid. He'd pushed his Harley to dangerous speeds on the empty dirt roads outside Liberty.

"Slow down or you're going to wipe out one of these days," Ted used to tell him. And Cole would grin and tell him to stop worrying, that he wasn't ever going to do anything their old man kept predicting he'd do.

He took the Jaguar into a hard left that would take him out to those dirt roads. Their father's predictions about both of them had turned out to be wrong. Ted was supposed to have become rich and successful. Cole was supposed to have ended up broke or worse. Instead, he'd managed to amass a fortune...and his cautious big brother had died penniless in a heap of twisted metal on a wet highway.

The irony was hard to believe. Life had taken the Cameron brothers in completely different directions...and one woman was the cause. If Ted hadn't married Faith, or if she'd at least been a true wife to him, he wouldn't have ended up on that road to Atlanta. He wouldn't have invested all his money in the market, either. It had to be costly to support a woman like Faith. Cole hadn't seen signs of it yet; she wore no jewelry except a simple wedding band, but surely she'd wangled more than that from his brother.

The girl who'd wept the time he'd brought her a single rose didn't exist anymore. The truth was, she never had. Sweetly innocent Faith Davenport had been a scheming opportunist. The name, the house...

A child his brother had put in her womb.

Cole downshifted to climb a steep grade. He didn't want to think about that. About Faith and Ted making love. About any other man caressing her, tasting her mouth, inhaling her fragrance. He was older now and a lot smarter. Life had taught him that love was just a synonym for lust and yes, it drove him crazy that she could still affect him, but that had always been her talent. She was more beautiful than ever, more desirable—and much more treacherous.

Why had she tried to keep Peter's existence a secret? It didn't make sense. The kid was her trump card. She must have known he wouldn't hesitate to toss her out, but throw his brother's son to the wolves? No way.

Cole drove faster.

You couldn't always figure out if a good poker player was bluffing. The only thing you could do to protect yourself was make the ante so high that the other guy had to back down.

The houses thinned on the outskirts of town, gave way, as they had before, to pastures and then second-growth woods. Cole shut off the air-conditioning, let down the windows, took a couple of deep breaths of air redolent of pine. The digital readout on the speedometer flashed higher and higher.

This time yesterday, he'd been in New York having drinks with his banker in a bar perched so high in the concrete canyons that peregrine falcons nested just above the window ledge. He'd sat there in his three-thousand dollar suit, drinking single malt Scotch while he enjoyed the view, the financial report…and the assessing glances of a stacked brunette at the next table. Liberty, Georgia, and everything in it—everything he'd left behind—could easily have been on a different planet. If he'd thought about it at all it had only been in terms of regret at having missed Ted's funeral…and of the pleasure he was going to get in denying Faith what she'd worked so hard to achieve. Ted's will, the pitiable condition of his estate, had played right into his hands.

But the game had changed. This wasn't about what had happened years ago, it was about the future. Peter's future. Ted had left his son penniless, and his widow's only talent lay in manipulating men for her own benefit. It didn't take a genius to figure out what the kid's life would be like.

Cole eased his foot from the gas pedal and pulled the Jaguar to the side of the road. A chorus of chitinous chirps and buzzes replaced the sound of the car's throaty purr. He clenched the steering wheel and stared out the windshield. Someplace along the way, late afternoon had given way to dusk. The first bright stars of the night sky hung over the valley, blinking like fireflies.

It was wrong. A child shouldn't have to pay for the mistakes of its parents, or for their failings, or for the untimely death of one them. Didn't he know that better than anybody? Peter was innocent. Kids always were, and they always ended up paying the highest price.

Darkness leached the last brushstrokes of color from the sky. The insect chorus rose to a new crescendo. He'd told Faith he'd be back in a couple of hours but it would take him longer than that. He had to make plans, come to grips with what those plans entailed...

Hell, he thought, and barked out a laugh, how was he going to do that?

After a long time, Cole sat up straight, started the car and headed back to town.

The evening had turned unexpectedly cool.

Faith sat, cross-legged, on a floor cushion before the fireplace in the den. She'd changed into jeans and a heavy sweatshirt, then built a fire to ease the chill. The flames warmed the room but they did nothing for the coldness that had seeped into her bones.

What a long, awful day it had been.

All her plans, her hopes, her dreams of making a new life for Peter, had been shattered. She couldn't blame Ted. He'd never intended to leave her and her son destitute. He'd talked a lot about Peter's future. Summer camp, when he was a little older. A private secondary school, in Atlanta. A top university and then a post-graduate degree.

"You've got him all grown up," she used to say teasingly, but she'd loved knowing her son would tread a path so different from hers, one free of uncertainty and poverty. So much for that theory. Planning never got a person anywhere. She should have remembered that.

A burning log slipped and tumbled onto the hearth in a shower of sparks. Faith uncrossed her legs and looped her arms around her knees. How was she going to tell Peter what lay ahead? That they had no money? No roof over their heads? He was just a child. He didn't understand the hatred that could blaze between adults, or the pain they could inflict on each other.

He could only endure.

Had he heard them shouting at each other? He must have because Cole hadn't been gone more than a few minutes when he'd come downstairs.

"Mommy?" he'd said. "Where's Cole?"

Her back had been to the door and she'd taken a few seconds to steady herself before she'd turned toward him. Her little boy's face had been solemn, his eyes dark.

"Cole had to leave, darling," she'd said. She hadn't bothered with the fiction of his returning in a couple of hours. Instead, she'd rattled off a story about unexpected business developments and forgotten appointments, but Peter hadn't bought any of it.

"He just went away?" he'd said, reducing her elaborate tale to basics. Yes, she'd said, because what else was there to say? "Oh," Peter had said, just that one soft word, but it was enough. His lip trembled and her heart almost broke.

"Come here," she'd said. "Give me a hug."

"No, thank you," her son had answered politely. And when she'd tried to make an occasion of the evening, suggesting they have an impromptu fried chicken picnic in front of the TV—a very special treat, because she never let him watch TV during mealtimes—he'd said, in that same courteous way, that he really wasn't very hungry and could he have P and J, instead?

Peanut butter and jelly had sound just about right to Faith, too. Comfort food, instead of a reminder that Cole had blown through her life again, the proverbial ill wind that did nobody any good. She'd dumped the chicken in the trash, made them sandwiches and chocolate milk, and Peter had gone quietly up to bed without saying more than a couple of words.

A log crackled as hot flames surrounded it. Faith sighed and stared into the flames as if they held the answers to all the questions in the universe.

Peter would get over what had happened. She'd see to that. She'd take him someplace special tomorrow. That big amusement park he liked so much, and to hell with the cost or the distance—and that was another thing to worry about. How would she get around in a town that had no public transportation, once her car was gone?

It wasn't really hers. Ted had leased it and if she wrote the check for the next month's payment, she wouldn't have enough left in the bank to buy groceries and pay the taxes due on the house in a couple of weeks. And, dammit, she had to pay those taxes, had to stay in this house until a judge ordered her out, had to, had to, had to...

She let out a breath.

What she needed was a lawyer who could stand up to Sam Jergen and his client. It wouldn't be easy; she knew that. The Cameron name—Cole's name, because nobody had ever really considered her a Cameron—still had meaning in this town. The couple of phone calls she'd made after she'd tucked Peter into bed proved it.

She'd called three attorneys Ted had listed in his phone directory.

"Hello," she'd said to the first. "My name is Faith Cameron. Mrs. Theodore Cameron. I'd like to stop by your office tomorrow and discuss—"

She hadn't needed to say more. The Liberty gossips were hard at work. A handful of hours had gone by but it seemed that everyone knew that Cole was back, that Ted had left him the house, that he'd left her an almost-empty checkbook.

"You want me to represent you in a lawsuit against your brother-in-law," the man said. "Sorry, but I'm full up."

The second asked, bluntly, how she expected to pay his fee. The third was no less subtle. "Mrs. Cameron," he'd said, "let me be as direct as possible. You can't afford me. And even if you could, what would be the point? Fighting your brother-in-law would be a waste of time. There's no way you can win. Not against him.''

"Why not?'' she'd said.

For some reason, that had struck the lawyer as wildly amusing because he'd burst into laughter before hanging up. To hell with him. To hell with them all. There were other lawyers out there, even if she had to go to Atlanta to find one who'd help her.

Faith yawned and rolled onto her stomach. The fire was warm, the sound of the crackling logs soothing. She knew there were things she should be doing instead of lying here. Draw up a list of attorneys from the phone book. Write down all the reasons she ought to be allowed to stay in Cameron House until she found work. Come up with a way to keep Alice because who else would take care of Peter once she found a job? Once she did, would she be able to afford the car payments or did it make more sense to give up the lease and buy something used?

She was so tired. Her body ached with weariness. A few minutes' sleep, that was all she needed. Just a few…

Faith's lashes drifted to her cheeks. Her breathing slowed and she fell into the darkness of a dream. Someone was weeping. The sound was terrible in its despair. A woman's voice, the sobs torn from the very depths of her soul.

Why? Why did he leave me?

The sobbing woman moved slowly through a landscape of swirling mist.

I loved him so much. I loved him with all my heart.

Faith moved slowly toward the woman. *Who are you?* she said. *Why are you crying for a man who never loved you?*

I don't know, the woman sighed. Somewhere in the distance, a bell began to toll. "I don't know," the woman said again. She raised her head. Faith saw her own face, her own eyes, her own wrenching sorrow…

Panicked, she jerked awake, heart thumping unsteadily as the dream faded. The fire had gone out, leaving the room dark and cold. And somewhere in the distance…

The doorbell was ringing.

Faith jumped to her feet and turned on the nearest lamp. The Limoges clock on the mantel began to chime nine in counterpoint to the bell. Who would drop by this late? Who would come by at all? Nobody came to visit the town pariah.

The bell stopped ringing as she hurried through the house to the front door, switching on lights as she went and hoping the noise wouldn't wake Peter. When she'd last checked, he was sound asleep, his teddy bear in the curve of his arm, his thumb tucked in his mouth. That had almost broken her heart. She hadn't seen him suck his thumb since he was two. He hadn't even done it when Ted—

The front door swung open just as she reached it. Faith cried out, stumbled back. A man stood in the opening, silhouetted by the light spilling from the foyer onto the porch. He was big, wide-shouldered...

"I rang the bell," Cole said. He stepped forward; she could see him clearly in the light but it didn't matter. Her pulse was still rocketing.

"You rang the bell and I didn't move fast enough to suit you, so you walked right in?" She spoke sharply, using her defiance as a shield. He'd scared her but she could feel something other than fear, something that had to do with the sight of him and the dream she couldn't remember.

"This is the second time you've broken into this house, Cole. I won't tolerate it again."

He laughed and brushed past her. "What will you do about it?"

Tight-lipped, she watched as he went toward the kitchen with the easy walk of a man who owns the ground beneath his feet. She had no choice except to close the door and follow him. He went to the sink, took a mug from the cabinet and filled it with the coffee she'd made a little while ago.

Her anger went up a notch. "Make yourself at home."

"Thank you." His courteous tone was as false as his smile. "I intend to."

Faith pushed up the sleeves of her sweatshirt. "All right, Cole. What do you want?"

He took a sip of coffee. "This is good." He smiled again.

She had an overwhelming desire to slap the smile from his face but instinct told her that she wouldn't get away with hitting him a second time. Instead, she dug her hands into her pockets and knotted them. "I'm pleased to see you have at least one practical talent."

She knew her face was turning hot. All the more reason to strive for a cool, detached tone.

"Answer the question, please. What do you want?"

You, he thought with a swiftness that was frightening. He'd seen the coolly elegant Faith this morning, the damned near-naked Faith this afternoon, but for reasons he couldn't begin to comprehend, this Faith in her sweatshirt and jeans, her hair loose and tumbling down her back, was the one that made him taut with desire.

He'd spent the last hour in a bar on the outskirts of town, a country gin mill where the bartender would probably have laughed if he'd asked for single malt Scotch. He'd nursed a couple of beers, listened to the saccharine tales of woe pumping out of the juke box, assured himself that what he was about to do was right, that he had no choice...that he didn't give a damn if his coldly clever sister-in-law liked his plan or not.

And that was the problem. She wasn't his sister-in-law, not in this getup. She was his girl, aged seventeen, all done up in oversize clothes because they'd gone swimming down at the lake one hot afternoon and afterward, the sight of her in her swimsuit, her nipples beaded with cold under the cheap polyester, had threatened to drive him out of his mind.

"Here," he'd said gruffly, and he'd taken his football jersey from the saddlebag on his Harley and handed it to her. "Put it on," he'd said, his voice low and hot, "before I come over there and rip that suit off you." And Faith had blushed and whispered maybe that was what she wanted him to do, even as she pulled on his shirt. He'd come up behind her then and, for the very first time, slid his hands under the jersey and cupped her breasts.

He turned away, cursing himself and the erection he felt straining against his jeans, and filled the cup with more coffee.

"Is Peter asleep?"

"Yes."

"Did he…" In control again, he swung toward her. "Was he upset?"

Her mouth thinned. "He's only a child, Cole. He's too young to know that some people say things just for effect."

"It wasn't like that. I…" He let out a breath, put the cup on the counter. "I'm sorry I disappointed him."

Faith shrugged her shoulders. "It isn't important."

"Of course it is." His voice took on an edge. "People shouldn't tell kids they're going to do things unless they mean it. And I did mean it, when I said I'd spend the evening with him."

Amazing, she thought. He sounded as if he really were upset. Well, maybe even Cole Cameron saw the difference between walking out on a woman and walking out on a child. After all, a lot of time had gone by, enough so he'd matured physically. Things had happened to him: his nose had been broken or something; there was a small bump halfway down its length. His body was lean and hard. He'd gone from being a beautiful boy to a handsome man. A gorgeous, dangerous man…

Stop it! she thought, and gave him a cool smile.

"I'll tell Peter you stopped by before you left."

"Did I say I was leaving, Faith?"

"Excuse me?"

"This is my home. Why should I leave it?"

"Because you don't live here." She took a deep breath. "I'm going to fight you for Cameron House."

"You'll lose," he said flatly. "That's if you can even find a lawyer to represent you."

Faith took her hands from her pockets and folded her arms over her chest. "I'll find one."

"Just be sure and tell him you can't pay him a retainer. Or do you have some money hidden away that you can tap into?"

"Once the house is mine, I'll sell it. There'll be enough money to pay legal fees and give Peter and me a fresh start."

"Ah. So, you're doing this for the boy's sake."

"Yes," she snapped, stung by the disdain in his smile.

"That's exactly why I'm doing it, not that it's any of your business."

"Move, just like that? Uproot Pete—"

"Peter."

"Uproot Pete from his home, his school, his friends, after he's just lost his father? Hell, Faith, I know the bright lights are probably beckoning, but maybe you should try considering the kid's needs, too."

"For your information," she said, her voice trembling, "Peter hates living here. He has no friends."

"Why not?"

"Because—because this is Liberty. I don't know where you've been the last years, Cole, but the town's the same as it always was. People gossip. They make judgments. When Ted was alive, they deferred to him but now that he's gone..."

She fell silent, but she'd said enough. He understood. Faith had dated _him_. He'd gone away and she'd gotten involved with his brother. That would have set tongues wagging but then she'd taken things a step further, gotten herself knocked up. Maybe that wouldn't be worth more than a raised eyebrow if the cast of characters had been different, but a hurry-up wedding between a Cameron and a Davenport would have been juicy news. In Liberty, it would probably stay news for the next hundred years.

"Hell," he said softly.

She nodded. "Exactly."

"And things have gotten worse since Ted's death, haven't they?"

"I guess you could say the gloves have come off. Peter doesn't get invited to anybody's house to play, or to go to parties. He's—he's pretty much an outcast."

"What you mean," Cole said coldly, "is that the boy is paying for your sins."

She looked up, eyes flashing. "You're a fine one to talk about sin. You left this town and never once looked back to see if I—to see if your brother needed you."

"Why would he, when he had you?"

"Damn you, Cole Cameron! You have no idea what my

life was like after you left. If it hadn't been for Ted—'' She stared at him, eyes blurred with sudden tears, knowing she'd been dancing on the edge of saying things she must never say. She swallowed the angry words, whirled away from him, grabbed a paper napkin from the holder on the counter and wiped her eyes. "This is senseless. The past is dead. The only thing that matters is the future. My son's future. And that future isn't in this godforsaken town."

"I agree."

Faith turned slowly and looked into Cole's face. "Do you mean that?"

"Absolutely." A muscle knotted in his jaw. "You're right. I'd forgotten what this town can be like. Give it some gossip and it'll worry it like a dog with a bone."

"Yes," she said quickly, "that's right. That's why I need to—''

"You need to bring the town to its knees."

She gave a quick, bitter laugh. "And pigs can fly. I can't do that, Cole. Ted could. Well, not really. Even he could only get people to pretend to accept Peter but—''

"I can."

She blinked. "You?"

"That's right." Cole leaned back against the sink, one foot crossed over the other, arms folded. It was a casual stance but there was a purposefulness to his posture, a flatness in his eyes that sent a warning tingle down Faith's spine. "What's the matter, baby?" His words were soft and taunting. "Don't you think I can make this whole damn town wish it had never heard the name 'Cameron'?"

Faith hesitated. "Look, all I want—''

"Did I ask what you wanted?"

"All I need is some money, just enough to get started somewhere." She drew a deep breath. "I'll make a deal with you."

He grinned, a quick slash of white teeth in his tanned face. "*You'll* make a deal with *me?*"

"You keep the house. I won't fight you for it. Just—just let Peter and me go on living here for a while, until I find a job. Until I sort things out…''

"Maybe I could let you live here until I sell the house," he said gently. "And then give you, say, fifty percent of the sale price. How's that sound?"

It sounded too good to be true. He was setting a trap. She knew it. She just couldn't figure out how to avoid stepping in it.

"Well," she said carefully, "that would be...it would be very generous. And—"

"And you'd be ever so grateful. Am I right, Faith?"

"I would be, of course. I mean—"

"You don't have to explain what you mean." Cole moved quickly. She thought he was going to walk by her and she started to get out of his way but he slipped his arms around her and even as she brought up her elbows and tried to jam her hands against his chest, his hand was in her hair, forcing her head back as he lowered his mouth to hers.

His kiss was a savage avowal of desire. She tried to tear her mouth from his but he wouldn't permit it. He used his teeth and tongue, penetrating her, forcing her to open to him. She hated him for it, hated him, hated him even as she moaned and let him bend her back over his arm and kiss her until there was nothing in the universe but the man who held her captive to his passion, and to hers.

He drew back first, ending the kiss even as her hands curled into his shirt. His hands clasped her shoulders; he held her out in front of him, his eyes blazing.

"My brother didn't have a chance," he said gruffly. "The poor bastard was lost the second you went after him."

"Get out of my house." Her voice shook. She could feel his fingers marking her flesh. "Get out!"

"We've had this conversation, remember?" She tried to wrench away from him again but he wouldn't let her. "I told you that you can't throw a man out of his own home."

"And I told *you*, I'm prepared to fight you in court. Everybody seems to think the Camerons are invulnerable. Well, not anymore. I know how the world works, Cole. Money is power. And the Cameron money is—" She stumbled as Cole suddenly let go of her. He dug out his wallet, removed a card and tossed it on the table. Faith eyed it with suspicion. "What's that?"

"It's the reason you're not going to fight me. Go on. Take a look."

She took the card from the table. Raised black letters were set on heavy ivory vellum. The design was understated, almost elegant, but she handled it with caution, as if it were a bomb that might go off.

"Read it out loud."

She took a breath. "'Cole Cameron.'" Her tone was hesitant. "'Cameron Oil. Cameron Exploration. Cameron Energy Resources. Cameron Invest...'"

"Investments," Cole said coldly, when her voice began to tremble. She looked up, the color fading from her face. "That's me, baby. Liberty's prize package. It's been an interesting nine years."

"Yes. So I—so I see. You've—you've gone into business."

He laughed. "Let's just say that I need this house and the three-quarters of a million it might bring the way a snake needs shoes."

Faith moistened her lips. "Then—then why...?"

"Why not let you have it? I could. I could burn the house to the ground, hand you a check for what it's worth and never once blink." He reached out, ran a finger down her cheek. She stared at him, mesmerized, and he remembered stumbling across a gazelle and a lion face-to-face in the desert. The gazelle had trembled with terror but the certainty of the outcome had kept it immobilized. "But I won't," he said softly, "because I know what you are."

"Cole. The past is dead. What I'm asking you for is Peter's future."

"Exactly. The boy is my brother's son. And Ted was my flesh and blood. I shouldn't have held him responsible for what you'd done. I loved him." His voice cracked; he drew a ragged breath. "Peter's a Cameron. So am I." His mouth twisted. "You're trash. You always will be."

"Damn you!" Tears of rage glittered in Faith's eyes. "Why

did you have to come back? I hate you. I hate you with all my heart!''

''That makes things simpler all around. We can dispense with the pretense.''

''I don't know what you're talking about.'' She stepped back. ''And I don't care. I'll manage without any help from you. Peter and I—''

''Peter's no longer your problem.''

''My problem?'' She laughed. ''He's my son. I love him. Is that beyond you to comprehend?''

''I considered throwing you into the street,'' Cole said calmly. ''It's where you belong. But I can see that the boy loves you. And that you love him, in your own way. So I'm going to let you stay around, Faith. You can continue to be his mother.''

''You're crazy.'' Faith whirled away and from him. ''You aren't God! You can't 'let' me continue to be my son's—''

''I'll do whatever is best for my brother's child.'' Cole turned her toward him. ''I don't just have money. I have friends. Powerful friends. They'd all agree that you're unfit to raise Peter.''

''You're bluffing,'' she said breathlessly. ''You couldn't—''

''You think so?'' He smiled tightly. ''Then call my bluff. See which of us comes out the winner. Me—or the woman who slept with me, then with my brother. Who got what she wanted and then drove my brother into another woman's arms.''

''You don't know how ridiculous that is!''

''Ted died on the road to Atlanta. The whole town knows why he was there, Faith, that you'd denied him the pleasure of your bed.''

Faith laughed. She couldn't help it. Nothing was funny but the laughter rose in her throat in one long hysterical wave and burst free. Cole's eyes turned to chips of green ice.

''Go on. Laugh. But I promise, you'll lose the boy...unless you cooperate.''

''Ah.'' She twisted free of his hands. ''Here we go. The

big bribe. 'Sleep with me, Faith, and I won't take your child from you.' Did I get that right?''

"Not quite." Cole's eyes locked onto hers. "I'm not asking you to sleep with me, baby. I'm telling you that you're going to become my wife."

CHAPTER SEVEN

FAITH looked at him as if he'd just told her he believed in flying saucers.

Cole cursed himself for being a fool. He'd intended to lead up to the idea, not drop it on her all at once.

He'd spent the past hours trying to figure out what to do about Peter. Offer to pay the boy's tuition at some classy boarding school? That would get him away from Faith's influence, all right, but the thought of sending such a little kid off to face the unknown made him uneasy. He wanted to help the boy, not hurt him.

He'd considered moving Faith and Peter out of Liberty to a place where he could keep an eye on them. New York, maybe, where his main offices were located. He'd find them an apartment, pay the bills, get the boy into a good private day school. Then he'd thought about the things Faith might do to fill her time. He'd phoned Jergen, who said she hadn't taken any lovers he'd heard of, but in a big city, without a man to ride herd on her, who knew what she'd do? Not that he gave a damn, personally. It was Peter who mattered, and he didn't want Peter raised in such an atmosphere.

Still, he had to do something. It was too late to walk up to Ted, put his arms around him and say he was sorry for the years of cold silence. There were times he thought his brother had been the only reason he'd made it through the first eighteen years of life. Ted had always been there for him. He could be there now, for Ted's kid. But how?

He'd sat in that bar, drinking beer, trying and trying to come up with a solution when some guy, already half in the bag, climbed onto the next stool and started whining about the difficulties of keeping a woman in line.

"A man's got to be on his toes," the guy had said, knocking

93

back a whiskey. "Can't trust a woman to do the right thing less'n he's watchin' her twenty-four hours a day. Can't even trust her to do the right thing with a kid."

That was when he began thinking about taking Peter away from Faith and raising the kid himself. What were the chances a court would let him do that? Zero to none, probably, but he had an office full of high-priced legal talent on retainer. Let the lawyers earn their bread wrestling with the problem. Not that a court battle would really provide a solution. The boy would still be living with his mother. She'd be his primary influence.

"Men ain't go no rights anymore," the guy on the next stool grumbled. "And thass dead wrong. A boy needs his dad to keep an eye on things."

"Yeah," Cole had agreed, even though his old man being around hadn't done him any good. But it didn't have to be that way. Ted had influenced Peter. You could see it in the way the boy behaved. He was a nice kid. But those days were over. Faith was in charge, now. Faith, not the boy's father. Not the boy's paternal flesh and blood.

It all added up. Peter needed a father. Faith needed a man to straighten things out in her life. Who could do any of it better than he? He shared Peter's blood. He knew Faith was a scheming bitch behind that angelic exterior.

Cole had tossed a ten-dollar bill on the bar, clapped the guy beside him on the back and told him to have the next one on him. He'd gotten into the Jag and while he drove to the house, he'd told himself there had to be some other way—and then he'd listened to Faith talk about Peter's life…

…*listened to her, and looked at her, and felt the old, hated stirrings of lust.*

To hell with that. He'd marry her because he had to. Because it was logical—but he should have kept quiet until he'd worked out the details. Then, maybe, she wouldn't be looking at him as if he'd lost his sanity.

"Excuse me?" she said, after what seemed like an eternity slipped by. "I thought—I thought you said…"

Her voice faded away. His first inclination was to fill the

silence by telling her she'd misunderstood. He could still back away from a plan that made his gut churn. No. There was too much at stake. He had an obligation to his brother's child and he'd fulfill it. So he composed his features and spoke as calmly as if he were laying out a new plan for one of his managers.

"I said that you're going to marry me."

She stared at him while the seconds dragged on. He'd wondered what her reaction would be, wondered what effect his words would have on her. What he hadn't figured was that she'd laugh.

"Marry you?" she said, gasping for breath. "You're asking me to..."

"Yes," he snapped, and she laughed harder. It enraged him. She'd have leaped at his proposal nine years ago. It would have been a commitment of love for him. For her, it would have been a ticket out of the trailer park.

What a fool he'd been, not to have seen through her.

"I'm not asking you," he said coldly. "I'm telling you. You're going to be my wife."

"Cole." Faith shook her head. "I know it's an old custom in some places, that a man is obligated to take care of his brother's wife by marrying her, but—"

"I don't give a damn for old customs and I sure as hell don't feel any obligation to you." He folded his arms over his chest. "My responsibility is to Ted. You're not fit to raise his son alone."

"Not fit to raise... What are you, a one man morality committee? You walked out of—of your brother's life. Let's not pretend you've suddenly turned into a paragon of virtue."

He jabbed his hands into his pockets, curled them into fists, told himself it would only make things worse to grab her and shake her.

"You were the reason for the trouble between Ted and me, you and your determination to snare a Cameron any way you could."

"And what woman wouldn't want that prize," she said sarcastically.

"Ted's gone. All that's left of him is his son. And, for Peter, all that's left of his father is me."

"Blood is thicker than water, right?" Faith folded her arms. "If it is, how come you didn't speak to Ted for years?"

"I was wrong. I admit it, I made a mistake—and I'm not going to make another. I'm going to see it that the boy is raised the way Ted would have wanted." He took a breath, then let it out. "If you think this through, you'll see that this is the right thing for Peter."

Her eyes narrowed. "And I'm sure *you'll* see why I'm telling you to take your feelings of guilt and stuff them. In other words, go to hell. I'd sooner marry the devil than marry you."

Faith stalked into the living room, plucked a throw pillow from the couch and punched it into shape. It was either that or punch him in the face. How could he stand there and tell her such a thing? Marry me, he said, as if he were king of the world and she were some pathetic peasant...

...And how could her heart have given the tiniest lurch, as if the years had rolled back and the man she'd once loved really was asking her to share his life?

His hand closed on her shoulder. "You're making this difficult."

"Am I?" She could feel her throat constricting. "Ah. I see. You thought I'd hear your little speech and tumble into a graceful heap, romantic that I am."

"I never took you for a stupid woman, Faith, but you sure as hell are being stupid now."

"Such is life. Console yourself with the thought that I'll look back someday and kick myself for turning down this magnificent offer."

"Let me spell it out for you, okay? You're broke. Your rosy future depends on fast-talking me into letting you stay on in this house—or convincing me to give you money so you can make that supposed new start. What are you planning? A crummy furnished room in Atlanta? A job flipping hamburgers? That's some hell of a life you've worked out for Peter, isn't it?"

It was a frighteningly accurate description of what she feared lay ahead but she'd never admit that to him.

"You've been watching too many old movies," she said coolly.

"Think about Peter. You claim to love him—"

"You—you son of a bitch!" Faith turned around and jabbed her finger into Cole's chest. "Don't you dare even suggest I don't love my child. He's everything to me."

"If that's true," Cole said softly, "then let me raise him as my son."

The words, so unknowingly uttered, almost ripped out her heart. The lie she'd lived all these years was turning to quicksand under her feet. She wrapped her arms around herself and took a step back.

"No."

A subtle change came over his features. A narrowing of his eyes, a tightening of his lips—she wasn't sure, exactly, she only knew that it frightened her.

"I can force you to marry me," he said softly. "Is that what you want?"

"What are you going to do?" It wasn't easy but she forced a smile to her lips. "Hit me over the head? Drag my body in front of a justice of the peace?"

"Very creative." He smiled thinly. "And tempting—but unnecessary."

"Really."

"Really." Cole tucked his hands into his back pockets and rocked back on his heels. It was a posture she remembered from years back, when he'd come up with something he'd figured was clever—like the first time he'd suggested parking at the lake instead of going to the movies.

Do you really want to see that James Bond thing? he'd said. *Because if you don't, I have a better idea...*

A better idea that had led straight to where she was now. Courage renewed, Faith lifted her chin.

"Perhaps you plan on hypnosis," she said politely. "I should warn you, I saw something on TV about hypnotism.

No matter how good you are, you can't make a person do anything she doesn't want to—''

"I can take Peter from you."

The words dropped into the room like stones. She stared at him, too stunned to answer.

"Did you hear me, Faith? I said—''

"I heard you. But you're wrong. He's my son."

"He's my brother's son, you mean."

"He's mine! And I'm finished listening to this—this crap! To hell with you, Cole Cameron! You come marching back into my life after all this time, talking about what's right and what's wrong—''

"How did my brother get involved with you?"

"That's none of your business!"

"Yeah. Yeah, it is, because I'm damn sure I know how it happened." Cole's mouth twisted. He grabbed her, shoved her back against the wall. "Did he come looking for you? Did he knock on the door one day and say, 'Hello, Faith, I'm Cole's brother and oh, by the way, if you ever need me for anything, just let me know'?"

She stared at him in dismay. He made it sound ugly but it was so close to the truth...

"I can see it in your eyes, baby. That's exactly what happened. Ted showed up, the innocent good Samaritan, and you squeezed out some tears or maybe you just sighed and said you were so lonely... God, how easy it must have been. My brother probably didn't know women like you existed. He'd have been a pushover, same as I was, even after my old man warned me what you were after."

"You father warned you about me?"

"Damn right." His eyes glittered with cruelty. "And I told him not to worry, that I'd get what I wanted without even singeing my fingers."

His words stung. It wasn't as if she hadn't figured out the truth a long time ago. It was just that hearing him say it made it so real...

"Well." She swallowed dryly. "I guess we deserved each other. You wanted what you got from me. And I—I wanted what I hoped I could get from you. Because it was all an act, Cole, every bit of it. I never loved you. Never!''

She fell silent, appalled by the enormity of the lie, wanting to call it back but knowing it was her only protection against him, even now.

"Honesty," he said, very softly. "At last."

"Why not? There's nothing between us anymore."

"You're wrong. There's Peter. He's the reason you're going to be my wife."

She stared at him in disbelief. "Are we back to that?"

"We never left it."

"Let me get this straight. You're prepared to enter into a mockery of a marriage because you feel a moral obligation to your brother's son?"

"This is a practical proposition. An arrangement that solves all kind of problems. You need money and a roof over your head. Peter needs a father."

"Are you sure it isn't payback? After all, I chose Ted over the great Cole Cameron."

Cole's face darkened. "You 'chose' him the way a spider chooses a fly. I was the lucky one. I got away."

"So we get married," she said coldly. "And everyone is happy."

"Peter will be happy. That's what matters. I'll love him as if he were my own."

Faith's heart lifted into her throat. "No."

"You seem to think I'm giving you a choice." Cole's mouth hardened into a flat line. "I'm not."

"Here we go," she said with forced lightness, "back to the unconscious bride scenario."

"If you force my hand, I'll take the boy from you. I'll go to court and sue for custody."

"You wouldn't," she said, her voice trembling. "Do you know what that would do to him?"

"I'm not an idiot, dammit!" Cole ran his hands through his hair. "I don't want to take him from you unless there's no other way." He hesitated. "I can see that he loves you. And that you love him."

"Am I supposed to thank you for that?" she said, with a bitter laugh. "For seeing that my child and I love each other?"

"I'm not pretending it's going to be easy."

"I'm amazed to hear it."

"People marry for worse reasons than a child's welfare, dammit!"

"Has it occurred to you that lots of children don't have fathers?"

"Lots of children aren't named Cameron. They don't have someone standing by, willing to take on the responsibility of raising them."

Faith laughed. "My God, how noble you are!"

"The boy is unhappy. You said so, yourself, that kids shut him out."

"That's why I want to move away. If I can start over—"

"Trailer trash is trailer trash, wherever you put it."

"You insulting bastard!"

"I'm being honest." His voice hardened. "If you won't put Peter's needs first, think about yourself. You'll get a much better payoff from this arrangement than you would have if Ted hadn't gone broke." His nostrils flared. "But I'm telling you up front, Faith, I won't let you keep me from your bed."

She stared at him. His jaw was set, his eyes steely. He meant every word. Fear made her knees threaten to give out, but she knew better than to let him realize it. If he sensed the slightest weakness, he'd strike like a cobra.

"I'm not seventeen anymore, Cole. I'm not some dumb kid from the wrong side of town you can scare with empty threats."

"You need to understand something about me, baby. I never make threats. I make promises."

"There isn't a judge in this country who'd take a child from its mother and give it to a stranger."

"I'm the boy's uncle. Hell," he said gruffly, "except for a quirk of fate, I could have been his father."

Faith's breath caught. She stared at him, heard his words echoing in her ears as the floor tilted. She reached out, seeking balance, and Cole's hands closed on her arms.

"Faith?"

Let go, she wanted to say, but she couldn't speak. The room was spinning; the world was going dark. She felt Cole lift her into his arms.

"Dammit," he said, "don't pass out on me."

Why not? she thought, and tried to laugh, but she couldn't. All she could do was wind her arms around his neck and bury her face against his shoulder, let his strength flow into her.

"Faith?"

Slowly, the word began to right itself. "I'm—I'm all right now," she said in a papery whisper.

She wasn't. He could see how pale she was, feel her trembling in his arms. Trembling as she once had when he held her, but then she'd trembled with passion, not with fear of him…except it hadn't been passion, it had been a lie.

He let her down slowly, telling himself not to think about the pliancy of her in his arms, the feel of her soft body as it slid against his.

"Sit down," he said briskly. "I'll get you a glass of water."

She shook her head. "I don't want any water. And I don't want to sit." She took a breath, raised her head and looked into his eyes. "Cole." Her voice was rough with emotion. "Cole, I beg you. Don't do this to me."

"Ah." He let go of her and flashed a smile. "I forgot how good you are at maidenly swoons."

What was the sense in telling him she hadn't been faking? All that mattered was making him see the insanity in what he'd proposed.

"Cole, please—"

"Don't waste your time, baby. You have a choice. Marry me and remain a part of Peter's life. Say 'no' and face me in court. It's up to you."

"How can you do this?" she whispered.

"Do what?" His eyebrows rose. "I'm offering to make you Mrs. Cole Cameron. I can think of half a dozen women who'd think that was a very generous offer."

"I'm not one of them."

"You were, at seventeen."

His words mocked her. He'd never believe that they were true, that she'd have married him when he was nobody, when he had no money...when all she'd wanted from him was his love.

"You're right. I'd have been giddy with excitement." She flashed a smile that was dazzling and, she hoped, careless. "But it had nothing to do with how I felt about you, Cole. Didn't you just tell me that? It was the name I wanted, not the man."

He took a step forward. An icy tremor danced along her skin when she saw the glitter in his eyes. "Be careful," he said softly.

"Why? What more can you do to me? You've already threatened to steal my son—" Dammit, her voice was shaking. *She* was shaking. She knotted her hands at her sides, forced herself to meet that insolent green stare without flinching. "You know what, Cole? I've had enough. Get out!"

"How come you're always trying to get rid of me?" His eyes moved slowly from her face to her feet, then to her face again. She felt as if he were undressing her, not with love or even with desire but as a show of power. Her cheeks burned with humiliation. "I can remember a time you used to beg me not to leave you."

"Another part of the act," she said coolly, and had the pleasure of seeing his eyes darken.

"Don't make the mistake of underestimating me, sweetheart." He took another step toward her. "I never lose a fight."

"That's because you fight dirty!"

"I fight to win, Faith. You'd better think about exactly what that means."

"I know what it means." Her voice trembled. "There are organizations that will back me."

"Sure. They'll turn Peter into a media sensation. That's one hell of a way of showing how much you love him."

"I *do* love him. And he loves me. Have you thought of that? How he'd hate you, if you tried to take him from me? How unhappy he'd be?"

"Kids adapt. And if he were unhappy, it would be your fault for not choosing to do the best thing for him."

"Just listen to you! You've taken your whole sick proposal and turned it on its ear." Faith glared at him. "*I'm* not the villain! You are."

"I don't think Pete will see it that way, not after I explain that all I wanted was for us to be one big happy family."

"Peter," she said, numb with pain, hating him with every beat of her heart, every whisper of her breath. "My boy's name is Peter." Her eyes met his. "And you're—you're despicable." Her voice shook. "I wish you'd never come back. I wish—"

He moved quickly, looped a hand around the nape of her neck. She dug in her heels but his grip was relentless as he forced her closer.

"You won't mind being my wife," he said roughly. "You'll still have the Cameron name. You'll have money. The only thing different is that this time, you'll want to be in your husband's bed."

Tears rose in her eyes and blurred her vision. Don't cry, she told herself, whatever you do, don't give him the satisfaction of seeing you cry.

"I'd sooner be in a convent."

Something flickered in his eyes. "Is that what you told my brother?"

"I'd never have said anything like that to him. I loved your brother!" That, at least, was the truth. Ted had been her best friend, the only person who'd ever shown her kindness.

"Did you?" Cole's voice hoarsened. "Tell me if you cried out in his arms, the way you cried out in mine."

"That was a lifetime ago. And it wasn't love. It was—it was sex."

He drew her, hard, into his arms. She tried to turn her face away but he tangled his fingers in her hair, forcing her eyes to meet his. "You're right. And the hell of it is that I've never forgotten how good it was. Answer me! Was it the same with Ted?"

She looked at him, this man she had once loved, and wondered what would happen if she told him the truth. The answer came in a heartbeat. He would never believe her. The past was a construct of lies. Too many lies, that cut too deep.

It was time for one last lie, to keep her safe.

"No," she said, "it wasn't the same with Ted. How could it have been? I didn't love you."

She cried out as his hand tightened in her hair. Hatred, raw and hot, blazed in his eyes.

"Love," he said, and laughed. "You don't know the meaning of the word. We're two of a kind, baby. We never let emotion get in the way of what we want."

"And you think my son's better off with you? With a man who has no heart?"

"Love for a child is different. It's the other kind that's a lie. The kind that makes a man think he wants one woman above all others, that makes him defenseless and weak."

"No," she said, but he'd already slid one hand down her spine, lifting her to him so that she could feel the heat and hardness of his aroused flesh.

"That's right," he said softly, reading her face, seeing the sudden bloom of color in her cheeks. "What men and women feel for each other hasn't a thing to do with love. I didn't understand that, when we were kids. I wanted you so badly I figured it had to be something special." He lowered his head toward hers until she felt his breath on her skin. "You taught me the truth, Faith. Love is just a word. Desire is what it's all about…and, damn you, I still feel desire for you."

He kissed her then, taking her mouth with greedy demand. His kiss was brutal but she didn't care. If anything, she welcomed the cruelty because if he'd been tender with her—if he'd been gentle…

Maybe he knew. Maybe he understood that she could want him and fight against the wanting only as long as he hurt her, because his lips softened, moved against hers in question instead of demand.

"Faith," he whispered, and suddenly it was a summer in the distant past when his kisses had meant everything, when she'd loved him. It broke her heart, to remember. And it made her want him with a desperation that drove everything else from her mind.

She made a little sound, one born of years of empty dreams, and wound her arms around his neck. Cole groaned, murmured her name again just the way he used to, as if it were the only word he needed or knew.

"Faith," he whispered, "open to me," and she did, oh, she did, she parted her lips, sought his taste, took his tongue into her mouth eagerly. He slipped his hand under her jeans, his fingers hot on her naked flesh, seeking out the heat and dampness he knew awaited him. She groaned, moved against his questing touch.

"Yes," she said, "yes..."

"Mom?"

The whispered word exploded into the silence. They broke apart. Faith swung around and saw her son standing in the hall in his pajamas, his hair tousled, his old teddy bear hanging from his hand.

"Mom," he said again, "what are you doing?"

Faith wondered what would happen if she admitted that she couldn't possibly answer the question, not even if she'd been the one who'd asked it.

CHAPTER EIGHT

COLE was the one who finally came up with a response.

"Your mother had—she had something in her eye." Pathetic, he thought, even as he said it, but it was all he could think of. It seemed to work. Peter looked in his direction as if he'd just realized he was there.

"Hey," he said happily, "you came back!"

"Hey yourself, champ. I told you I would, didn't I?"

"Did you have a bad dream, sweetheart?" Faith held out her arms and tried not to think about what might have happened if Peter hadn't come downstairs. "Is that what woke you?"

"Uh-uh. I just thought I heard voices…" He grinned. "And I did," he said, and launched himself past her to Cole, who caught him and swung him around.

"How you doing, Pete? You okay?"

"Sure. I'm fine." The boy hesitated. "You said you'd watch that movie with me."

"I know." Cole set the child on his feet. "I'm sorry about that. I should have called to say I'd run into some problems."

Peter beamed up at him. "That's okay. You couldn't help it, right?"

"Right," Cole said easily.

Wrong, Faith wanted to say. Don't put your trust in this man, Peter. But she smiled instead and held out her hand. "Come on, sweetheart. I'll take you back to bed."

"Would you like some cookies?" Peter said, ignoring her. "Mommy always lets me have some, when I can't sleep."

"Sounds like a great idea."

"Peter." Faith cleared her throat. "Sweetheart, it's awfully late. And Mr. Cameron was just leaving."

"I'm s'posed to call him Cole. And I already invited him to have milk and cookies."

"He's just being polite, Peter. He doesn't actually want—"

"Sure I do." Cole ruffled Peter's hair. "I love cookies. Especially... I don't suppose you have Oreos, do you?"

Peter grinned and reached for his hand. "The double kind," he said.

Faith watched the man and the boy walk away. After a few seconds, she followed them to the kitchen, stood by stiffly as Peter got out the milk, two glasses and the Oreos. Cole swung him onto a stool at the counter, then sat down beside him. I might as well not be here, she thought, as she watched her child listening, enraptured, to the lies spewing from the lips of the man she hated.

"I'm sorry I didn't get back to see that video, Pete. I got caught up in business but I promise, it won't happen again."

Peter nodded and said he understood. But he didn't, Faith thought bitterly. How could an eight-year-old possibly understand that Cole would lie whenever it suited him? Not that it mattered. Cole could have brought the house down around their ears and her son would have found a way to explain it. Her little boy was knee-deep into hero worship of this stranger...except, he wasn't a stranger. He was the man who'd fathered him.

"Peter!" She spoke more sharply than she'd intended. Both of them looked at her and she knew she had to be careful. She was dancing on the edge of sanity. If she wasn't vigilant, she'd give the whole thing away. "Peter, sweetheart, I want you to go back to bed now."

"Aw, Mom—"

"It's okay." Cole touched the tip of his finger to Peter's nose. "Besides, we're going to be seeing a lot of each other from now on."

"No," Faith said quickly.

"Yes." Cole didn't bother looking at her this time. "How does that sound?" He hoisted Peter into his arms. "Would you like us to spend more time together?"

"Oh, yeah. How about tomorrow?"

"Sorry, Pete. I'll be busy—though I will see your mom tomorrow night. I'm taking her out for the evening."

"No," Faith said again, with an edge of hysteria in her voice. Neither the man nor the boy looked at her.

"Just you an' her?" Peter said.

"Just the two of us, yeah. Grown-up stuff, champ." Cole put the boy back down on the stool. "Nothing you'd enjoy but I promise, you and I—"

"Don't do that," Faith snapped. "Don't lead him on when you know none of this is..." She caught her breath. Her son was staring at her and she forced herself to calm down, to smile and speak gently. "Peter, darling, go upstairs now. I'll come tuck you in in a few minutes."

"But I want to stay here with Cole."

"Hey, champ. Do as your mother says, okay?"

"I don't need you to intercede on my behalf," Faith said stiffly.

"Go on," Cole said, as if she hadn't spoken. "It's late."

Peter sighed. "Okay."

Cole plucked the boy from the stool and swung him in an arc before putting him on his feet. "Good night, Petey."

"Cole?" Peter smiled shyly. "You can give me a hug, if you want."

"Peter," Faith said, but it was too late. Cole bent down and caught the boy in his arms. His eyes met hers over the top of the child's head. "You don't want to be shut out of this," he said softly. "Do you?"

"Shut out of what, Mom?"

"Hush." Her voice trembled but there was nothing she could do to stop it. She reached out, caught Peter as he started past her and hugged him hard. Too hard, probably, but she couldn't help it. He gave her a questioning look and she flashed a quick smile. "Go on," she said. "Back to bed."

Her son trudged up the stairs. She waited until he disappeared down the hall and she heard the faint sound of his bedroom door closing. Then she looked at Cole, knowing she mustn't beg, knowing she could do nothing less.

"Please," she said. "Don't do this. You *can't* do this."

"Of course I can." He walked slowly towards her, put a finger under her chin and tilted her face up. "I can do anything I want. You'd better accept that." He bent his head, brushed his mouth over hers. "I'll see you tomorrow night. Eight o'clock, at the inn by the lake."

"If you think I'm going to be there tomorrow or any other time—"

"Your choice, baby. If you'd rather discuss our wedding plans here, that's fine with me."

Faith clamped her hands into fists. "I hate you. I just hope you—"

Cole kissed her again. When he finally lifted his head, his eyes glittered. "Eight o'clock, at the lake. You do remember the lake, don't you, Faith?"

Before she could think of an answer, he was gone.

At ten minutes before noon the next day, Faith drove into a parking lot just off a busy Atlanta thoroughfare. She pulled into an empty space, shut off the engine, flipped down the sun visor and looked at herself in the mirror.

It wasn't a reassuring sight.

She rarely wore makeup, nothing but a little mascara and lip gloss, but today she'd done her best to live up to the headlines that trumpeted Make Yourself Into A New You in the slick women's magazines. After a sleepless night, "a new you" sounded like a pretty good idea. She'd applied foundation, blusher and lipstick...

So much for the wonders of makeup.

The blusher and lipstick only made her pallor more pronounced, the violet smudges of exhaustion under her eyes more visible. It was a look that might have gone over well on a high-fashion model but it only made her look sick.

She grimaced, plucked a tissue from the center console and wiped off as much of the stuff as she could. That was better. Now she just looked like something the cat had dragged in. With a sigh, she opened the door and stepped from the car.

What did it matter, how she looked? What she said, how she said it, would be what counted.

She had an appointment with one of Georgia's best-known family law attorneys. Her job would be to convince Elmore Bookman to represent her. He had the expertise and he wouldn't be intimidated by the kind of legal talent she suspected was at Cole's fingertips.

Bookman's name had popped into her head in the middle of the night. He'd been all over the papers a couple of years back when he'd won a seemingly impossible custody battle between a wealthy grandfather and the child's far-from-perfect mother. The mother's saving grace had been her love for the child but the evidence of her promiscuity had been overwhelming. The pundits had been sure the girl would lose the case. Bookman had laughed at the skeptics. The mother would win, he'd said, and she had—thanks to her attorney.

If anyone could see to it that she kept Peter, Elmore Bookman could.

Faith located Bookman in the Atlanta telephone directory at 4:00 a.m., fell into exhausted sleep at five and awakened at seven. She phoned the lawyer's office, hung up on a machine that told her that Bookman, Rigby and Goldman began their day at nine and placed the call again, at nine-oh-one. After talking her way past a receptionist, a legal associate and Bookman's secretary, she'd finally heard the attorney's booming voice on the line. He'd listened, interrupted her after a couple of sentences and said he had fifteen minutes free at noon. Could she make it?

Faith glanced at her watch as she stepped from the elevator that had whisked her to the twelfth floor in the glass-and-steel high-rise. It was three minutes of twelve. Ahead, double doors bore the name Bookman, Rigby and Goldman in raised black script. She took a deep breath, opened the doors and walked into a small, elegant reception room.

"Mrs. Cameron to see Mr. Bookman," she said, when the receptionist looked up.

"Of course, Mrs. Cameron. Won't you be seated?"

She was too nervous to sit very long but she didn't have

to. A silver-haired woman appeared, smiled and held out her hand.

"I'm Leona. Mr. Bookman's secretary." She led Faith down the hall to a large corner office. "Mr. Bookman will be with you in a moment. May I get you something while you wait?"

Courage, Faith thought. "No, thank you," she said. Carefully, she crossed her legs at the ankles, lay her purse in her lap and folded her hands on top of it. "I'm fine."

She wasn't. By the time the door opened again, her stomach was on a roller-coaster ride. Suppose Bookman laughed at her story? Suppose he told her she was wasting his time?

The attorney did neither. He was a pleasant, distinguished-looking man who took notes as Faith told him about her brother-in-law appearing after an absence of almost a decade and threatening to take her son away. When she'd finished, Bookman raised steel-gray brows.

"Because?"

"Because he thinks I'm—I'm unfit to raise my child."

"And are you? Unfit to raise your child, Mrs. Cameron?"

Faith colored. "I most certainly am not."

"I see. In other words, the gentleman wants to take your son for no reason you're aware of?"

She hesitated. "I'm aware of the reasons," she said softly, "but they're untrue."

Bookman nodded. "And those reasons are?"

"He—he believes I won't set a good example for my child."

"Because?"

"Because—look, this is very complicated."

The attorney smiled politely. "Uncomplicate it then, Mrs. Cameron."

Faith moistened her lips. "This goes back a long way. The, uh, the problems between..." Cole was her brother-in-law. Why was it so difficult to call him that? "For one thing," she said, after a moment, "he believes I coerced his brother into—"

"Your deceased husband?"

"Yes. He believes I coerced him into marriage."

"And did you?"

She shook her head. "No. No, I did not."

"And that's your brother-in-law's reason for thinking you're not fit to raise his nephew?"

His nephew. His nephew...

"Mrs. Cameron? Is that why he thinks you're not a fit mother?"

Faith got to her feet. It was hard, saying these things under a stranger's penetrating stare. She walked slowly to the window.

"There's more to it, Mr. Bookman. As I said—"

"It's complicated. But if you want me to help you, you'll have to tell me more. So far, I can't imagine why this man would even think he could get custody." The attorney scrawled a note, then looked up. "Could he bring witnesses to testify that you're an unfit mother?"

Faith thought about her housekeeper. The townsfolk of Liberty. The rumors and the gossip. She cleared her throat.

"I suppose it's possible he could get people to say things... But they wouldn't be true!"

"Would you have witnesses to refute that testimony?"

She walked to a chair, sat and looked down into her lap, at her folded hands. "No."

"I see."

"No," she said again, and looked up at the attorney, "you don't see! He's wrong about me. The people in town are wrong. Look, I know how this sounds but—but that's why I've come to you, Mr. Bookman. I need a lawyer who can take a difficult case and win it."

Bookman pushed aside his notebook, capped his pen and tented his hands on the burled-walnut desk.

"Mrs. Cameron, so far as I can tell, there is no case. Your brother-in-law has threatened to fight you for custody of his nephew. I'll be happy to send him a letter, explaining that his chances of winning such a fight are virtually nil." He smiled.

"That is, if you can assure me your brother-in-law can't prove you're either a child molester or a serial killer."

Faith tried to smile in return. "I promise you, I'm not. But you don't understand. He'll pursue the case no matter what you tell him. He'd do anything to hurt me."

"Because?"

"Because…because he thinks I denied my husband…" She colored. "That I denied him intimacy. And—and—"

"And?" Bookman prompted.

"And we were—we were lovers, years ago."

"You and your brother-in-law?"

"Cole and I. Yes. But we were very young, and—"

"Cole?" Bookman sat up straight in his chair. "Surely you don't mean Cole Cameron? *The* Cole Cameron, of Cameron Oil?"

Faith nodded. The attorney had gone from looking polite to amazed. Her heart sank. That couldn't be a good sign.

"Well! That does put a twist on things."

"Does that mean you won't represent me?"

Elmore Bookman chuckled. "I'd be delighted to represent you, my dear. There's nothing I like better than doing legal battle with the best hired guns around." His smile faded and became a thoughtful frown. "As your counselor, however, I'm obligated to point out several things."

"Such as?"

"Cost, for one. If Mr. Cameron is committed to fight you to the bitter end, the costs would be high."

"How high?"

Bookman shrugged. "Six figures."

"Six…?" She put her hand to her throat. "Are you serious?"

"I'm afraid I am."

"Don't you do *pro bono* work, Mr. Bookman? You said yourself, you'd love to take on the best—"

"Our firm sets priorities." He spoke gently but firmly. "I'm afraid the senior partners have agreed on the cases we'll try, free of charge, for the next several months."

"Then I'll pay you. Not all at once but so much per month."

"Mrs. Cameron, there's another factor involved you need to be aware of." The lawyer pursed his lips. "I get the feeling there are things you haven't told me about this situation. No." He held up his hand. "No, don't divulge anything more. It's true, whatever you'd say would be covered by attorney-client privilege but if you're not going to go ahead with this case..."

"I haven't said that."

"You were uncomfortable telling me about your prior relationship with Mr. Cameron, and about his charges concerning your intimate relations with your husband."

Faith blushed. "Yes but surely you can understand—"

"Indeed I can, but it's only fair to warn you that such things would come under close scrutiny. Mr. Cameron's attorneys would delve deep into your life. It's the way this kind of action develops. The other side learns all your secrets." Bookman's voice gentled. "*All* of them, my dear, I can promise you that. A man like Cole Cameron has the resources to do it."

All her secrets. Faith began to tremble. The truth about Ted, which she had sworn never to reveal. The truth about Peter, which she didn't dare reveal because then she *would* lose her son...

She rose swiftly to her feet and held out her hand. "Thank you for your time, Mr. Bookman. I'm sorry if I've wasted it."

"You're not going to go ahead with this, then?"

"I—I can't."

"If you wish, I'll be happy to write that letter for you, free of charge. I doubt it will change Mr. Cameron's mind, but—"

Faith shook her head. "It won't. And—and I have another option."

"What?"

She hesitated, knowing how it might sound. "Mr. Cameron has—he's asked me to marry him."

Elmore Bookman started, then began to laugh. "Well, that's the most unusual *quid pro quo* I've ever heard of. Legal lingo that means 'this for that,' Mrs. Cameron. A trade-off, if you will. So, if you marry the gentleman he won't sue for custody?''

"Exactly."

"In that case, what you really need is a prenuptial agreement. You know, a document that will guarantee you certain things if the marriage should fail."

If it should fail, Faith thought, and almost laughed. It was doomed to fail but then, it wouldn't really be a marriage.

"I suspect Mr. Cameron will want you to sign one, also. Men of his wealth generally do and in a case such as this..."

Bookman's words trailed away but Faith knew what he meant. Cole didn't love her, didn't trust her, didn't like her. He'd surely want her to sign a document that would keep her from getting her hands on anything that was his.

"Still," the lawyer continued, "you're entitled to safeguard yourself."

"Ask for money, you mean?" Faith shook her head. "I don't want anything of Cole's. Not one penny."

"Well, then, consider the matter in reverse. Is there anything of yours you'd want to keep from Mr. Cameron? We could draw up a prenup that would protect you."

"The only thing I have that he wants is my son." She held out her hand. "Thank you anyway."

Bookman rose and shook her hand. "Goodbye, Mrs. Cameron. If you should change your mind about that protective prenup—"

"I'll call. Thank you again. Goodbye."

The elevator was waiting. Faith stepped inside and pressed the button for the lobby floor. Her hand shook as she did it. Cole had won. She'd known he would, she just hadn't wanted to admit it.

The lobby was cool. She could see waves of heat rising through the huge glass windows. She paused, unwillingly to face either the heat or the reality of what awaited her, Cole and dinner and the acquiescence he'd expected all along.

There was a coffee bar on the opposite side of the lobby and she headed for it instead of the door. Her head was pounding. She'd skipped lunch. Breakfast, too, now that she thought about it. A couple of aspirin, a large cup of black coffee, maybe even something sugary and caloric might make her feel up to the drive home.

She ordered a doughnut and coffee. Paper plate in one hand, paper cup in the other, she sank into a chair at a corner table. She took a sip of coffee, looked at the doughnut...

Bile rose in her throat. She shoved the doughnut away, drank some more coffee and then pushed it away, too. She propped her elbows on the little table and rubbed her hands over her eyes.

What now?

Now, Cole got what he wanted, that was what. Her child, who already acted as if she were an afterthought in his affections. And he got her. Not that he wanted her as a man should want a wife. He'd made that clear. He wanted her in other ways.

Her pulse began to race.

No matter what he believed about her, he wanted her in his bed. He'd said it, admitted it in the way he'd touched her, kissed her.

Is there anything of yours you'd want to keep from Mr. Cameron?

"The only thing I have that he wants is my son," she'd said, but it wasn't true. Cole wanted her sexually. Not to make love to. To humiliate. To subjugate. To use.

We could draw up a prenup that would protect you.

Faith sat very still. After a long moment, she blotted her lips with a napkin. She got to her feet, collected her trash, carried it to the receptacle and dumped it in.

The elevator ride up to the floor that housed Bookman, Rigby and Goldman seemed interminable but, eventually, the doors slid open. She stepped from the car and went through the double doors to the reception desk. The woman behind it looked up, raised her eyebrows and smiled.

"Did you forget something, Mrs. Cameron?"

"No. It's just—I'd like to see Mr. Bookman again."

The receptionist looked doubtful. "Well, I'll ring his secretary, but I don't know…"

"He said to call if I wanted to reconsider a suggestion he made. If I could just see him for a minute or two…"

Moments later, Faith stood in the attorney's office. "I've reconsidered," she said. "I'd like you to draw up a prenuptial agreement for me."

Elmore Bookman sat down at his desk. "That's an excellent plan, my dear. If you'll give me the name and address of Mr. Cameron's attorneys…"

"What for?"

"So I can arrange to meet with them. We'll need to get some idea of his total worth… Why are you shaking your head, Mrs. Cameron?"

Faith knotted her hands together in her lap. "I don't want that kind of agreement. I want the other one you mentioned, the one designed to protect me from—from having Mr. Cameron gain access to—to my personal property."

The lawyer sat back and folded his hands on his desk. "I see."

Faith could tell that he didn't. He looked puzzled. Well, why wouldn't he be? She'd made it clear that she had nothing to safeguard. No money. No property.

"There is something I have that Mr. Cameron wants."

"In that case, let me get my secretary in here. She can set up an appointment so you and I can discuss—"

"I was hoping you could write the document now, Mr. Bookman. It will only have one clause."

"Just one?"

"That's right." Was the air draining out of this room? Faith felt as if it were. She took a couple of shallow breaths. "I want you to make it clear that I will have sole custody of my son, should Mr. Cameron dissolve the marriage for any reason. In exchange for that, I'll agree to function as his wife in all possible ways except—except—"

"Yes?"

"…in all possible ways except that I won't be intimate with

him.'' Faith saw the stunned look on the lawyer's face, felt
the heat rising in her own, but her voice, at least, was steady.
''I want it written into a prenuptial agreement, Mr. Bookman.
I will never, not as long as I live, have Cole Cameron in
my bed.''

CHAPTER NINE

AT DUSK, Cole stood on the balcony of his suite at the Liberty Inn and looked out over the water to the jack pines that lined the curving shoreline.

He was no stranger to the lake. He knew the shore and all the little tucked-away coves the trees hid. When he was a boy, he'd ridden here on his bike to fish for trout, though he'd never caught anything more exotic than a catfish.

In his teens, he'd come out here with Ted. They'd drink beer and have what they used to call Deep Talks about the Future. Mostly, Ted had talked and he'd listened, because the future had never looked terribly fascinating.

Once he bought the Harley, he came to the lake even more often, almost always with a girl seated behind him, her arms wrapped tight around his waist. There were lots of places far from the bright lights of the inn where a boy and a girl could explore the mysteries of each other's bodies.

But after he brought Faith here, he'd never come with anyone else. Those balmy nights. Faith, breathless with excitement and nerves. Him, wanting her so badly he ached. He'd take the blanket from the motorcycle's saddlebag, spread it on the grass and lie down with her in his arms. Then he'd kiss her. Touch her. Every inch of her, turned on by the little sounds she made, by her innocence, by the way she'd put her hand over his as if to stop him from exploring her secrets and then how she'd slowly, so frustratingly slowly, loosen her grip and let him stroke her until they were both trembling on the brink of completion…

"Hell," Cole said, and turned his back to the lake.

Great. Just great. Faith would be here any minute and what was he doing? Getting himself worked up as if he were a stupid kid instead of a man who understood that some women would do anything to get what they wanted.

He took a cold ale from the minibar, opened it and tossed the cap into the wastebasket. He tilted his head back and took a long, cooling drink as he walked onto the balcony again.

The town had changed in the past nine years. There was a monster shopping mall out toward the highway and a fancy coffee bar on Main Street, but the old saying was true. The more things changed, the more they remained the same. The inn was still handsome, the town center still small. The residents of Liberty, the ones who'd lived here when it was still a sleepy village instead of an Atlanta suburb, were as clannish as ever—and gossip among them was still the town's life force.

He'd forgotten that until he checked in the other night. A clerk with an artificial smile handed him a key and a kid wearing the red jacket with the inn's logo on the pocket grabbed his one piece of luggage.

"This way, sir," he'd said.

Cole hadn't needed the kid's services. He preferred to do things for himself, but he'd once spent the Christmas holidays doing just what the kid was doing. His motorcycle had died; he'd been short a hundred bucks for the needed parts to bring it back to life. Every tip had counted—he could still recall how it felt, each time some dude pressed a dollar bill into his hand. So he'd let the boy lead him to his room and do his thing, opening the French doors onto the balcony, pointing out the view over the lake, turning on the air-conditioning, turning off the air-conditioning...

"That's okay," he'd said quickly, when the kid started to explain the phone system. "I used to work here."

"Yeah?"

"Yeah," he'd said, smiling. "I lived in this town once upon a time." And he'd put a bill a lot bigger than a dollar into the boy's hand.

Big mistake.

"Wow," the kid had breathed.

Wow, indeed, Cole thought as he watched a sailboat catch the wind down on the lake.

In New York or London, in the financial capitals of the world, a bellman would have accepted the generous tip without blinking. In Liberty, the boy had probably told the story to a dozen people within the next hour. By the end of the day, Cole figured there wasn't a person in town who didn't know he was back and with money in his pocket.

"You didn't tell us you were *the* Cole Cameron, sir," the desk clerk had gushed.

"Yeah," Cole had replied, with a grin. "Well, that's because I've always been *the* Cole Cameron."

The joke had fallen flat on its face. "Absolutely, sir," the clerk had said. "And we're proud to have you stay at our establishment."

For a man who valued privacy, it was an uncomfortable situation. You could be relatively anonymous in a big city, but not here. Everybody in town had something to sell him and the kid who'd handled his luggage popped up at the door like clockwork to see if there was anything he wanted. Cole finally had to ask the clerk to screen his calls, the kid to back off.

He lifted the bottle of ale to his mouth and took another drink.

He had to admit, the irony was incredible. At eighteen, he'd been the town pariah. Now he was the town celebrity, Liberty's claim to fame in the big world beyond its borders. Too bad his old man wasn't around to see it. Or the sheriff. Or even Jeanine Francke, who'd framed him, but he'd done some discreet checking and learned her husband had thrown her out on her butt years ago. Too bad. How he'd love to have shoved his success in their faces...

His throat tightened.

And how he wished he could share it with Ted. His brother had always believed in him. He'd been the one positive force in his life. They'd loved each other, relied on each other...until first Cole, then Ted, had fallen under the spell of a witch.

Cole put the empty bottle on a small table, then curled his

hands tightly around the wrought-iron balcony railing. Faith might as well have been a witch, the way she made a man blind to the truth, but she didn't need black magic. All she needed was that beautiful face and lush body. That sweet, hot mixture of innocence and sensuality. She'd always been able to turn him on.

She still could. One look, and he'd wanted her. He'd taken her in his arms, kissed that silken mouth until it heated under his, until she'd made that soft sigh that used to drive him out of his head with longing.

Cole stood straight. She was good at what she did. Well, so was he. Her specialty was men. His was risk, not so much of assets but of situations, and the course he was about to take proved it. He'd be part of Peter's life—he loved the boy already. He'd give him what he needed, the love and direction a good father should provide. Faith would be a good mother. He had to admit, she obviously loved the kid. With a man to keep her in line and pay the bills, she'd bring Peter up right.

He went back into the sitting room and took a document from the coffee table. He'd phoned his attorney late last night and explained what he wanted, a prenuptial agreement but with certain specific provisions. Ray Foss had tried to disguise his surprise but it had crept into his voice.

"You're sure?" he'd said.

Cole had assured him that he was, although he couldn't fault the man's reaction. The request for a prenup on such short notice had been unexpected enough but the provisions he'd insisted on were, he knew, harsh. The prenup spelled out the generous benefits Faith would reap from being a faithful, dutiful wife but it also made it clear that she'd lose everything, including whatever money or possessions she might have gained through the marriage, if she didn't live up to the letter and spirit of the agreement.

"No settlement sum?" the lawyer had asked.

"None," Cole had replied.

"I don't think you can really do that, Cole. No court in the country would—"

"I can do whatever I choose," Cole had said crisply.

"Whether or not a court would uphold my right to do it is a different story. Draw up the document and get it to me by tomorrow morning."

The people who worked for him all knew better than to ask for explanations but Ray had been with him for a long time. He'd persisted, suggesting Cole might want to pull back a little, take a day or two to think things over. He hadn't said it like that, of course; instead, he'd talked about the importance of meeting to discuss Cole's plans, the future, what he'd called the overall intent of the prenup.

"The overall intent," Cole had replied bluntly, "is to make sure my blushing bride understands that the gravy train stops if she ever decides to walk out of this marriage. I'll expect her to be like Caesar's wife, entirely above any kind of suspicion, as long as she belongs to me."

"Belongs to you?" his attorney had repeated with caution.

Cole had silently cursed himself for the slip. He hadn't meant it. He certainly didn't want Faith to 'belong' to him...*although she would, whenever they were alone in the bedroom...*

"A poor choice of words," he'd said briskly. "I meant that I want to ensure her compliance. Do you understand, Ray? Can you draw up such a prenup and do it fast?"

Ray could. He did. The document, delivered by messenger this morning, a seemingly endless list of Draconian whereases and wherefores, had put a grim smile on Cole's lips.

He was sure Faith would turn pale at the sight of it.

"Sign this," he'd say, and she would because she had to, but she'd know she was turning her life over to him...

And that they would set the night on fire each time he took her in his arms.

Cole felt his body stir. He took a breath, expelled it, and waited for the moment of truth to arrive.

The clerk at the reception desk was leafing through some papers and barely looked up when Faith approached him.

"Yes?"

"Cole Cameron's room, please."

"Mr. Cameron has the Lakefront Suite. Who shall I say is…?" The man looked up, eyes widening. "Oh. Mrs. Cameron. How nice to see you."

"Thank you." She'd never seen him before, not that she could recall. "What floor did you say the suite is on?"

"The fourth. Mr. Cameron is expecting you. Let me ring for a boy to show you—"

"No," she said quickly. "That's all right."

"It will only take a minute."

"Thank you, but it's not necessary."

She saw the clerk reach for the phone as she started toward the elevator. He was probably phoning Cole to tell him she was on her way. On her way, she thought, like a ritual sacrifice to the altar.

The elevator was old and slow. That was fine. She was in no rush to see Cole or to deal with what lay ahead. *If* it lay ahead. She'd had time to think, on the drive back from Atlanta. Elmore Bookman had confirmed what she'd already suspected. Cole couldn't get Peter from her. He could only tie the both of them up in an endless legal knot. Increasingly, she doubted if he really intended to go ahead with what he'd threatened.

A man wouldn't deliberately marry a woman he despised. If he did, though, her insurance lay inside the shoulder bag swinging against her hip with every stride.

A small brass plaque pointed the way to the Lakeside Suite. Faith started down the corridor, past a wall of mirrored glass panels that reflected her image in seemingly infinite number. Nervously, she smoothed down the skirt of her white cotton dress.

I should have worn jeans, she thought, *just to show Cole how little I think of this meeting…* and then the door at the end of the corridor swung open and she saw him waiting, and her heart almost stopped because he was—there was no other word for it—he was magnificent.

No finely tailored suit. Not today. Cole wore chinos, a navy cotton shirt with the collar open and the sleeves rolled up. He was incredibly handsome and dangerously masculine, and in that one instant Faith knew that she had never stopped wanting him, that in some dark, terrifying way she couldn't begin to comprehend, a woman might want a man and despise him at the same time.

She came to a halt, her pulse hammering so loudly that she half expected he could hear it, too.

"Faith." His voice was low-pitched, rough around the edges. There was a dangerous glitter in his eyes, a tension around his mouth as he stepped forward. She wanted to turn and run, but she couldn't. He thought he had her right where he wanted her and the last thing she could afford to do was show him any weakness. It was bad enough she'd melted under his kisses last night, but it would not happen again. Her body had betrayed her with this man nine years ago and that betrayal had changed her life, forever.

"Cole," she said, pleased with how calm she sounded. She smiled politely and continued toward him. He stepped aside and she took what felt like a final breath before she moved past him into the suite and the door swung shut after her.

He gestured toward a blue silk sofa flanked by a pair of matching chairs. Faith ignored the sofa and took one of the chairs. Cole leaned against the balcony door, his feet crossed at the ankles, his hands tucked into his pockets. He stood so close to her that she had to tilt her head back to look at him. It was vaguely discomforting and she suspected he knew it.

"How is Peter?"

She moistened her lips with the tip of her tongue. "He's fine."

"You haven't told him our plans, have you?"

Her spirits lifted. That sounded hopeful, as if he was going to admit he'd only been bluffing. "No," she said, "no, I haven't."

"Good. I prefer breaking the news to him myself."

"Then—then, you're really going to—to—"

"To force you into this marriage?" He smiled coolly. "That's how you see it, don't you, Faith?"

"You gave me an ultimatum. You told me what you'd do if I didn't agree. How would *you* see it?"

Cole sat down on the sofa, took a handful of papers from

the coffee table and held them toward her. "I'd call it an opportunity," he said. "Perhaps you'll agree, once you've read this."

Her hand shook as she took the papers from him. Stop, she thought furiously. She could feel Cole's eyes on her as she tried to read the words on the top of the first page but she was too upset to see them as anything but an incomprehensible jumble of symbols.

"It's a prenuptial agreement," he said.

She looked up, caught by the purr of anticipation in his voice. He was smiling, though his eyes still held a dangerous gleam.

"Of course," she answered, as if men handed her such things every day of her life. She looked down again and began to read.

Cole had thought of everything. Her life had been planned in meticulous detail, legal paragraph after legal paragraph. She'd expected a prenup that would detail what she wasn't entitled to, but this one began with the things he would provide her.

Clothes. Jewelry. All her personal needs to be charged to his various accounts. Additional accounts, if she required them, to be opened in his name. So many dollars per month to be paid into a checking account, the sums to be reconciled by his accountants every three months. He must have seen her pause at that because he said, pleasantly, that surely she could understand the requirement.

"I have no intention of permitting you to stash away a little nest egg of your own," he said. "I'm sure you see the need for that."

The coldly vicious explanation combined with his obvious intention to treat her like a well-paid but little-trusted concubine enraged her. She thought back to that moment in the hall when she'd imagined herself still wanting him and she wanted to laugh but she'd get that chance, soon enough. She could wait.

"Oh, yes," she said, "yes, I do."

Faith continued reading. On page three, the agreement detailed what he would expect of her. She would travel with him. Act as his hostess. Organize his household staff.

She looked up. "You left out the details of how you want me to mother my son," she said politely. "You know, supervise his baths, his bedtime, check his homework...or are you willing to trust my judgment?"

Cole smiled. "I'm willing to grant you your maternal instincts."

"Thank you," she said, even more politely, and returned to the document.

On page four, she discovered what she would get if she ever ended the marriage.

Nothing.

And what she would get if she ever had an extra-marital affair.

Nothing, again.

And how Cole would have her declared unfit to raise Peter if she did either.

"What if you choose to end the marriage?" she said, lifting her head and looking at him.

"I won't."

"Or if you have an affair?"

"I won't do that, either."

"I see. Am I expected to take that on face value?"

"Yes," he said, without hesitation, "you are. Perhaps you've forgotten the reason for our marriage, Faith. I intend to provide a moral, stable home for Peter. I couldn't do that, could I, if I divorced you? Or if I slept around."

"No. No, you couldn't. Sorry. I guess I forgot what a great moralist you are, Cole. Silly of me."

A muscle knotted in his jaw. He watched her as she continued reading the agreement. He kept waiting for her to look up and ask if he really thought he could get away with this, but she didn't. When she'd finished, she put the papers on the table and looked at him.

"Fine."

He tried not to let his surprise show. "You don't want to discuss anything you've read?"

"No."

"Did you understand it all?"

"Oh, I think so." Faith folded her hands in her lap. "You've made it clear that you're prepared to buy my fidelity, that you have no respect for me, and that you expect me to find it impossible to behave honorably. Would you say that about sums it up?"

She smiled, though he thought he saw a flash of pain in her eyes. For a second, he felt a fist close around his heart but then he remembered her lies, the way she'd used him and Ted, and the feeling was gone.

"Yes," he said coldly, "it does. Then, you'll sign?"

"I will."

"Good." He reached for the phone. "I've arranged for a notary and two witnesses."

"Not yet."

Cole sat back. Here it came. What would it be? Delicate tears? Heart-wrenching sobs? Her face lifted so that he'd see the glint of despair in her eyes? Or would she be more direct, give him a look that promised everything a man could possibly want if he showed her just a little bit of generosity?

He felt his body quicken.

He might, if she played her part right. If she moved onto the sofa beside him, if she wound those slender arms around his neck...

"Cole?"

He blinked. Faith had taken a document from her shoulder bag. A legal document, judging by the dimensions of the single sheet of paper she held out to him.

"What is that?" he said.

She smiled, but he could see the piece of paper shaking in her outstretched hand. "It's *my* prenuptial agreement," she said softly.

Of course. He should have expected as much. She had more than a sexy body, she had a good mind. Even in the days when he'd done his thinking with his hormones instead of his head, he'd admired her intelligence. Okay. He took the paper from her. Why not read whatever she'd come up with? A good laugh might restore his equilibrium. That he'd even contemplated showing her any charity proved that he'd come close to losing it.

"Your prenup," he said. "You went to see Jergen?"

"No. What would be the point? You probably own him."

She got to her feet, tucked her hands into the pockets of the white cotton dress. The simple action made her breasts press lightly against the thin fabric. He could see the pebbling of her nipples. He knew it wasn't his presence that caused it—he had the air conditioning on and the room was cool—but the sight sent a message straight into his groin. He forced his eyes down but that was a mistake. Now he was looking at a long expanse of tanned legs and trim ankles shown to their best in slender-heeled sandals with straps that looked as if they were made of gossamer.

Cole could almost feel the electricity hum in his blood. He stood up, irritated as much at himself as he was at Faith.

"What'd you do? Write this yourself?"

"I went to Atlanta," she said calmly. "And I met with an attorney who handles things like this."

"Ah." He really had forgotten that quick mind of hers. He smiled coolly. "Let me guess. You told him who I am—"

"Of course."

"And he said, 'Why, my dear Ms. Cameron, you've stumbled into a goldmine.'"

Faith didn't laugh, didn't even smile. She looked at him, her eyes giving nothing away. "What he said doesn't matter. All you need be concerned with is what *I* said to him."

Cole nodded. "I can imagine."

"I doubt if you can." She jerked her chin toward the paper he held in his hand. "Read it."

How much would she ask for? He looked down, read the numbingly effusive tumble of legal language. Would she want a hundred thousand? Five hundred thousand? A million or more? He toyed with the idea of letting her have the money. He could add stipulations. She'd get a lump sum of so much if she warmed his bed each night for five years, so much more after ten...

And then he reached the single paragraph that mattered. No legal mumbo jumbo, just plain words in plain English. Faith Davenport Cameron agreed to perform all necessary wifely duties save one.

She would not have sexual relations with her husband.

He stared at the paragraph, at the neatly printed spaces beneath it, ready for his signature and hers. And he began to laugh. Really laugh, great roars of laughter that echoed through the room.

"I'm glad you find this so amusing."

He looked at Faith. Her face was white, her eyes pools of darkest blue. He began to speak, laughed instead, and finally caught his breath.

"I hope you didn't spend a lot of money on the services of this attorney," he said. "Where'd you find him? On a street corner?"

"It's a legitimate document," she said in an icy voice. "From a respected law firm."

Cole chuckled. "So, is this their idea of a joke?"

"It's my idea of respectability. I know you're the one who thinks he has the moral high ground, but even a woman you believe has no ethics—a woman like me—will only stoop just so far."

Her words wiped the smile from his face. Her sarcasm shouldn't have meant a damn but it got to him anyway, which was crazy. He was doing the right thing. He knew it.

"This isn't worth the paper it's printed on," he said, and tossed the document on the table.

"If you mean it's unenforceable in a court of law," Faith said quietly, "you're probably right."

"There's no 'probably' about it." He moved quickly, grasped her wrists. She jerked back but he brought her arms up, held her fists against his chest. "Marriage involves sex, Faith. You can't expect me to sign a document that says it doesn't." He transferred his hold on her wrists to one hand, slid the other slowly down her spine. "Sex is an implicit part of marriage."

"It won't be, in ours."

"Do you really expect me to agree to that?"

She didn't know what she expected, not anymore, not with his hand moving against her back, with his body hard and warm against hers.

"Yes," she said, her voice shaky, "I do. Ours is nothing but a marriage of convenience."

A marriage of convenience. If anybody had asked him, he'd have laughed at the term and said it was straight out of the eighteenth century. A man didn't take a beautiful woman as his wife and then not sleep with her.

Cole bent his head, inhaled the scent of Faith's hair. Lavender, maybe, or just summer sunshine. Whatever the aroma, it was as out of date as the concept of a marriage of convenience.

"Don't—don't do that," she said.

"I'm not doing anything." It was the truth. Burying your face in a woman's hair, nuzzling the silky locks from her throat and brushing your mouth against her satiny skin didn't qualify as "anything," not in a world where men and women tumbled into bed almost as easily as they shook hands. "Not a thing," he said, his voice hot and low. "Nothing you could actually call 'sex.'"

Couldn't you? If this wasn't sex it was the next best thing to it. Faith felt as if her heart might burst.

"I mean it, Cole. I won't have sex with you."

Color striped her cheeks; her eyes were wide and glittering. Her lips were parted. Won't you? he thought, as she trembled in his arms.

"If you insist on this marriage," she said, "it will be without intimacy."

Without intimacy. Such an old-fashioned phrase. The amazing thing was that it sounded right, coming from her. If he hadn't know what a little schemer she was, he'd have believed her. But her body, her voice, even the way she looked at him, gave her away. She could say she wouldn't have sex with him but sex was what she wanted. What she needed. It was what they'd always wanted and needed from each other.

He thought about telling her that, about telling her what she could do with the agreement…and then he thought of what it would be like, once they were married, to make her admit that only place she belonged was in his bed.

It would be easy.

His body hardened at the thought. She responded to it. Her breath had quickened; her skin was turning hot. He could take her now and she would let him, despite the silly prenup, despite what she claimed. He could take her and plunge deep inside her…but he wouldn't. He wanted time for a slow seduction, that kind that would, at last, rid her of the power she held over him.

Cole let go of her. "I'll sign it," he said calmly, and reached for the paper.

Moments later, both prenups had been signed and properly witnessed. With what seemed terrifying speed, Faith found herself on a private jet headed for Las Vegas. Cole had made all the arrangements, including asking Alice to spend the night at the house so she could baby-sit Peter.

A handful of hours later, Faith stood before an altar hung with artificial flowers while a stranger in a shiny blue suit said the words that made her Cole's wife.

CHAPTER TEN

FAITH wondered if she'd broken some kind of record.

She'd been married twice, each time to a man named Cameron. She hadn't wanted either marriage, though it had been easier exchanging vows with Ted. Maybe it was because she'd felt affection for him. Or maybe it was because Ted hadn't been any sort of threat.

Cole was.

He'd signed her version of a prenup but she didn't trust him. He'd given in far too easily and then there was that unsettling moment when he'd taken her in his arms and insisted that kissing her throat, drawing her against the hardness of his body, wasn't sex. Perhaps it wasn't, by a dictionary definition, but what he'd done had made her ache for more.

Yes, he was a threat. No, she didn't trust him. She didn't even trust herself. She thought about that when he slid a plain gold band on her ring finger. Looking down, she'd half expected to see "Property of Cole Cameron" engraved on the polished surface.

"By the power vested in me by the State of Nevada," the man who'd married them said, and it was done. She was married to Cole.

He didn't waste time on niceties. She was grateful for that. No smile, certainly no attempted embrace. He shook the justice's hand, took her elbow and led her to the limousine that had taken them from McCarran Airport to the wedding chapel.

"I've told the pilot we'll head straight back to Liberty," Cole said. "I want to get there before Peter wakes up, so we can break the news to him before he hears it from anyone else."

Faith looked at him. "Who could possibly know?"

"By now? Probably half the town. I explained the situation

133

to Alice and asked her to keep quiet but I suspect she won't honor the request.''

"She won't honor it at all, if it concerns me.''

"What?''

"Nothing.'' Faith took a deep breath. "You told Alice we were getting married? Before I'd agreed?''

"There was never any question.'' He looked at her, his smile filled with arrogant self-assurance. "You just needed time to accept the inevitable.'' Then he picked up a newspaper, opened it and began to read.

Angry tears stung Faith's eyes. Two wedding ceremonies, and she'd wanted to weep through both. It had to be a record, just as she had to be the only woman in the world forced into loveless marriages twice by the same man.

They reached Liberty just as the town began to stir. The ride to Cameron House in Cole's Jaguar was a continuation of the silence that had fallen between them since the ceremony, hours before. When they arrived, Cole stepped from the car, opened Faith's door and held out his hand. She thought of running past him, up the porch steps without looking back. Maybe then all of this would go away. It was stupid, she knew, but she'd clung to the desperate hope that once they were back in Georgia, he'd tell her that the charade was over, that he never expected her to live up to the agreement she'd signed and that he was returning to wherever it was he'd come from...

"Faith?''

She looked up. His eyes burned into hers.

"Yes,'' she said, and she ignored his hand, got out of the car and made her way to the porch. Alice opened the door before she could take out her keys.

"Good mornin', Mrs. Cameron.''

Faith nodded as she stepped into the foyer. "Good morning.''

"Makes it easy on everybody around here, don't it? Not havin' to call you by a different name, I mean.''

Faith felt her face fill with heat. I ought to be used to it, she thought. Alice had always been condescending. Ted had told her to ignore it and she'd done her best, but the situation had never been comfortable. Now it would be even worse.

"Now that you mention it," Cole said pleasantly, "I guess it does." He stood beside Faith, his arm around her waist. His body, his touch, were a strong, comforting presence. "And that's what we all want, Alice, don't we?"

The housekeeper's gaze flickered with uncertainty. "I expect so."

"I'm glad we agree. In that case, I think this would be as good a time as any to discuss your future."

"My future, Mr. Cameron?"

"I'd like you to decide if you want to stay on here, or if you'd be happier working for someone else."

Alice jerked back in astonishment. "Why, I've never considered—"

"Consider it, then," Cole said, his voice hardening. "I know you're fond of Peter and that he's fond of you but I'll make other arrangements, if things aren't easy for *everyone* around here. Have I made myself clear?"

The woman swallowed. "Yes, sir. You have."

"Good." He smiled. "How is Peter?"

"He's fine, sir. Still sound asleep."

"We'll let him sleep, then, while you make us some breakfast."

"I never eat breakfast," Faith started to say, but Cole ignored her.

"Do you still make those great biscuits?"

Alice's smile softened. "Yes, sir, I do."

"That's what we'll have, then. Your biscuits, scrambled eggs, bacon and coffee. Lots of coffee." He looked at Faith. "How does that sound, darling?"

"I told you," she said stiffly, "I never—"

"Well, you will, today. It's the start of our honeymoon."

He swung her up into his arms. Caught off guard, Faith gasped and struggled to free herself. Cole only held her tighter.

"That's all right," he said softly. "Alice understands. Don't you, Alice?"

"Yes, sir. Uh, Mr. Cameron?" The housekeeper's voice

followed them up the stairs. "The boy from the hotel brought over that suitcase. I put it just where you wanted, in—"

"In our room," Cole said softly, just loud enough for Faith to hear. "Right where it should be."

Faith held her tongue until he'd elbowed the bedroom door shut. Then she pounded a fist against his shoulder.

"Put me down!"

"My pleasure," he said, and dumped her on her feet.

"What kind of performance was that?"

"A necessary one."

"It was ridiculous!"

"Use your head, Faith." Cole's carryall stood in the middle of the floor. He picked it up and put it on the bed. "Alice would wonder what was going on if we didn't behave like newlyweds."

"She's wondering what's going on as it is." Faith glowered at him. "What do you think you're doing?"

"I'm getting undressed."

God, he was! He pulled his shirt out of his trousers, opened the buttons. The shirt landed on the bed. On *her* bed. She stared at Cole's wide, muscled shoulders that flowed into powerful biceps; the hard chest with its inverted vee of chestnut hair. Her mouth went dry. She didn't want to remember, didn't want to feel those emotions ever again.

"Stop it!"

His brows rose. "Excuse me?" It sounded polite but it wasn't. The words, the look on his face, were a challenge.

She glanced at his shirt lying on her bed. "This is my bedroom!"

"It's our bedroom, baby. Get used to it."

"I am not sharing a bed with you, Cole. You signed an agreement—"

"Do you want this town to think you're my wife or don't you?"

"Frankly, I don't care."

"Peter will care." Cole's eyes narrowed. "Besides, I saw how Alice treated you."

"Oh, that," she said, as if it didn't matter.

"Yeah. Oh, that." His voice sharpened. "You're my wife. I won't tolerate anyone showing you disrespect."

Maybe he was human, after all.

"That's generous of you," she said carefully, "but I—"

"Generous, hell." He walked through the bathroom, opened the door on the far wall and peered into the small study that adjoined it. "You're mine, now."

"Yours?" she said incredulously. "*Yours?* I don't belong to anybody, Cole Cameron. You'd better get that straight."

He strode back toward her, caught her by the shoulders and took her mouth with his. She felt the power of his kiss, the heat of it...and hated herself for the soft moan she couldn't prevent. Shaken, she could only stare at him when he finally lifted his head.

"You're mine," he said roughly. "Sooner or later, you'll admit it. And when you do, I'm going to collect." He picked up his suitcase. "Until then, I'll bunk on the sofa in the other room."

Casually, he strolled into the bathroom and shut the door. Faith snatched his shirt from the bed and hurled it at the wall. It didn't help but there wasn't time to vent her anger any more than that. As soon as she heard the sound of the shower, she stripped off her clothes and changed to shorts and a cotton shirt. She was brushing her hair when a tentative knock sounded.

"Mommy?"

Peter. She dropped the brush on the dresser. She wasn't ready to face him yet...

"Mom? Can I come in?"

Faith took a deep breath. "Yes, of course, darling," she said brightly, and flung the door open. He son looked at her, then peered past her into the bedroom.

"Is he here?"

"Cole?" She could feel her smile tilt and she fought to keep it on her lips. "Yes. Yes, he is. Peter. I have... I mean, we have something to—to tell you..."

"What your mother means," Cole said, from just behind her, "is that we got married last night."

"Married? You and my mom?"

"Uh-huh." He put his arm lightly around Faith's shoulders. "I apologize for not telling you about it but we made the decision kind of fast. We figured we'd surprise you."

Peter stared at him. "Alice said there'd be a surprise but I never figured…" He looked at Faith. "Mom?"

"Nothing will change," she said quickly. "Not for you."

"That's right, champ." Cole dropped his arm from her shoulders and squatted on his haunches. "So, what do you think? Will it be okay? Having me around, I mean?" He cleared his throat. "I understand it might be tough. You loved your father a lot, and he loved you. But I'll love you, too—if you'll let me."

The boy's lip trembled. "A lot?"

"Yeah." Cole cleared his throat again. "A whole lot."

"As if you were my father?"

"Exactly as if I were your father."

Panicked wings seemed to flutter in Faith's breast as her son smiled and went into Cole's arms. He could never know the truth, she thought desperately. Never—or he would do as he'd wanted to do all along. He'd go to court, sue for custody of Peter…

And win.

The summer days drifted past, one merging, unnoticed, into the next. And as they slipped by, Faith lost hope that Cole might remove himself from her life.

Didn't he have things to do? she finally said, when she came down the stairs one morning and found him waiting for her in the dining room. Someone else to torture? Ultimatums to issue? An empire to run?

That made him laugh. "An empire, huh?" He pushed back his chair, enjoying the sound of the legs scraping against the wooden floor. His old man would have cuffed him a good one had he done such a thing when he was a kid. "I can handle things from here. For a while, anyway."

For how long a while? Faith wanted to ask, but she could see the answer for herself. He'd had two more telephone lines brought in; a fax machine, a computer and a couple of printers had been installed in the library. Cole was settling in for the duration and Peter was enthralled. Her son had become Cole's shadow.

At first, she'd tried to keep him from barging into the library. She didn't much care about Cole's privacy. Her concern was for Peter. He'd done that to Ted, who'd used the library as a home office, too. Ted never turned him away; he just ignored the intrusion. Faith would go searching for her son and find him sitting quietly on the leather sofa, or playing on the floor with a toy.

"Sorry," she'd say, and Ted would look up and smile as if he hadn't noticed...which was fine. It was just that there'd been times she'd seen the lonely look on Peter's face and it made her heart ache, knowing that her little boy was trying for a relationship Ted just couldn't provide.

Cole was different. "Hey, champ," he'd say, when Peter scooted through the door. "How're things going?"

He'd take a few minutes to talk with him. Sometimes, he'd put aside what he'd been doing altogether. Faith was startled the first time she found the two of them on the floor, laughing as they zoomed toy cars over the Italian tile.

"Peter," she'd said gently, "don't bother Cole. He's busy."

"Actually," Cole replied, "Pete's doing me a favor. I was looking for way to get off the phone with Paris, and he gave it to me." He grinned at the child. "Right, Pete?"

"Right," Peter said, grinning back.

Faith started to protest but what was the point? She was Cole's wife. She'd agreed to abide by his rules and anyway, she'd never seen her little boy happier. Denying him these moments would be selfish. As the days slid by, she found herself wondering what would happen if her son found out that the man he was starting to love was really his father.

When she caught herself, she was horrified. It was a terrifyingly dangerous way to think. She could not permit such thoughts...but then she'd hear the two of them engrossed in an earnest discussion of the latest Braves game, or what was going to happen to the Falcons when football season started. She'd find them laughing over a Monopoly board on a rainy afternoon. She'd watch as two hands, one small, one large, dipped simultaneously into a bowl of salted popcorn with what Peter called just a wisp of sugar added because, it turned out, both of them preferred it that way.

Her heart, her pathetic, sad heart, filled with happiness. Faith told herself it had nothing to do with the fact that Cole was her son's father. She'd have been happy if any other man—a Scout leader, a teacher, a baseball coach—put a smile on her boy's face, but she knew it wasn't true. And then she'd do her best not to think at all, because she knew that neither Cole or Peter could ever know the truth.

Gradually, she found herself drawn into the things they did together. She tried not to get involved. The less time she spent with Cole, the better. But it was hard to say "no" to Peter when he begged her to go fishing with them so she could see that he'd learned to bait his own hook; it was selfish to say she'd rather read than go outside and laugh her way through a game of ball that had rules the two of them obviously made up on the spot.

What woman would want to sit alone with a book when the boy you loved and the man you'd once adored were having fun together?

Nights were more difficult. Faith knew they looked like an average family. They had dinner. They watched TV. They read, they listened to music. They did all the things other people did. She and Cole even managed polite conversation, for Peter's sake. But then Peter would go to bed—they took him up together and tucked him in—and when they returned to the living room, the silence of the night would settle between them.

She began going to her room early. "Good night," she'd say politely.

Cole would look up, his eyes dark and unfathomable. "There's no need to leave on my account," he'd say, his voice cool now that there was no need for pretense.

"Oh," she'd say, "I'm not. I'm just..." Tired. Sleepy.

Headachy. She had lots of excuses. Then she'd climb the stairs, conscious every step of Cole's eyes on her, just as she'd be conscious later of his footsteps outside her door, of the sound of the shower running in the bathroom...of the beat of her heart as she imagined herself rising from her bed, stripping off her nightgown, opening the door and going into the shower with him, imagined putting her arms around him and lifting her face to his while her breasts pressed against his water-slicked skin and his mouth claimed hers.

He thought about it, too. She was sure of it. She caught him watching her one evening, his look hot and hungry. She felt her entire body flush with heat and when she stumbled through another pathetic excuse and went to her room, she fell back against the closed door, breathless.

Would this be the night? Would he open the connecting doors and come to her bed?

She sank down in a chair. If it happened, she'd turn him away. She'd married him and yes, she was his wife and yes, she'd only fault herself if she gave in to desire and made love with him...but it wouldn't be love, it would be sex, and she'd never have sex with him. Hadn't she told him that? Hadn't he agreed to it? He'd even signed that prenup.

Except—except they both knew the document was meaningless, that he'd only signed it to humor her or maybe to humor himself, because he was positive he'd be able to change her mind. He hadn't tried, and she hoped he wouldn't. Because if he came to her in the night, if he woke her by kissing her, if she felt his hands moving on her body, she would stop him. She would stop him...

Wouldn't she?

When she finally fell asleep, she dreamed of Cole, of lying in his arms, of laughing with him, walking with him, doing all the things they'd never been able to do when they were young. She awoke, exhausted, a little after eight. She showered, dressed, went downstairs and found Cole and Peter waiting for her. The man and the boy exchanged a private smile.

"Hi, Mom."

"Good morning, Faith."

She looked from one face to the other. God, she thought, oh, God, this was so hard. They had the same eyes. The same smiles. The same noses, except for that little bump in Cole's...

"How'd that happen?" she said, without thinking.

"What?"

"That bump in your nose. It wasn't there when..." She flushed. "when you were younger."

"Oh." He grinned and rubbed a finger over the spot. "Let's just say I had an argument with a piece of heavy equipment and the equipment won."

"Like Billy Cullen," Peter blurted. "He had an argument with a roller coaster. I mean, about a roller coaster. I mean, with his sister about a roller coaster. And he banged up his knee."

Faith looked at her son. "What on earth does Billy Cullen's sister have to do with a roller coaster?"

Peter shot a sheepish look at Cole who sighed dramatically and reached for the boy's hand. "It seems the Cullen kid went to Six Flags, argued with his sister about whether or not she was brave enough to ride the Mind Bender..."

"The what?" Faith said, and laughed.

"It's a roller coaster," Peter said excitedly. "Billy says it's huge. Billy says we should ride it unless we're chicken. Billy says—"

"Cole says it's time to stow it, champ," Cole said, and grinned. He looked at Faith. "We thought we'd go to the amusement park today." He cleared his throat. "And we hoped you'd come with us."

No, she thought. Thank you for asking but don't be silly. Go by yourselves. I'm not big on amusement parks or roller coaster rides or—or on spending the day with you, Cole, pretending we're a family when we're not...

"Faith?" Cole said, and she looked into his eyes, saw that he wanted her with them, that he really wanted her with them, and the floor seemed to tilt under her feet as she said yes.

They shrieked with terror on the Mind Bender and the Ninja, and laughed when they got soaked riding the Log Flume. Faith

said she'd rather walk on hot coals than ride the Georgia
Scorcher and after watching that coaster for a while, Peter said
well, he'd ride it for sure, except he didn't want to leave his
mom standing around while he did and Cole said, solemnly,
that sounded exactly like what he'd been thinking.

They ate hot dogs and drank soda, and when the long, wonderful day ended, they drove home through the soft, warm
night, Peter sound asleep in the back seat, Cole and Faith
saying little but, perhaps for the first time, not needing to find
ways to fill the silence.

"I'll carry him up," Cole said softly, when they reached
the house.

Faith nodded. "I'll get the door."

Peter awoke just long enough to mumble a protest when she
undressed him and got him into his pajamas. He needed to
wash his hands and his face, still sticky from cotton candy,
and she knew he ought to brush his teeth, but she looked at
her sleeping child, smiled and decided that one night of bad
habits wouldn't end the world.

"Good night, sweetheart," she whispered, and kissed his
forehead.

"Good night, son," Cole said softly, and Faith's throat
closed up.

They tiptoed from the room, shut the door carefully behind
them. Faith looked at Cole. The day was over. It was time to
go to her bedroom and leave him behind but she didn't—she
didn't... Her heart skipped a beat. Oh, she didn't want to...

"Did you have a good time?" he said quietly.

She smiled. "Wonderful."

He reached out a hand, gently touched it to her nose. "You
got sunburned."

"So did you."

Cole cleared his throat. "Faith. I want to discuss something
with you."

"Yes?"

"Let's go downstairs."

What could he want to tell her that would make him sound
so serious? The warm joy of the day faded. She knew what it

was. This—this sojourn was coming to an end. Of course. He'd been here, what, almost three weeks? He'd been sweet to Peter and polite to her and now he was returning to the real world. His world. Peter would miss him. Just Peter. Only—

She blinked as Cole switched on a living room lamp. "I didn't think I'd enjoy being back here," he said. "In Liberty, I mean."

Faith turned and looked at him. She smiled politely. "I understand."

"But these weeks have been..." He hesitated. "They've been great."

"Yes. Yes, they've been—pleasant."

His eyes darkened. "Pleasant? Is that the best you can do?"

"I don't know what you expect me to say, Cole. I mean—"

"Never mind." He ran his hands through his hair, paced away from her, then paced back. "Peter's been happy."

"Very. And—and I want to thank you for that. He's really—really connected with you, Cole, and—"

"He's had a tough time, Faith. You told me but I didn't realize..." Cole took a breath. What the hell was the matter with him? He had something to tell her and she'd be happy about part of it. As for the rest—as for the rest, what did it matter if it pleased her or not? She was his wife. She had certain obligations. "I've managed to change things a little."

"I know. And—and I want to thank you for that, too. Taking him fishing, bike riding, going to those ball games with him—"

"Dammit, Faith!" Cole glowered at her. "What are you thanking me for?" His voice roughened. "I love the kid. I couldn't love him more if he were my own."

She nodded, afraid to speak, afraid words that might betray her would come tumbling from her mouth.

"What I meant, about changing things... Pete says the other kids are treating him better. Maybe that's the wrong way to put it. I get the feeling he's been accepted."

Faith nodded again. He had been, and it was all Cole's doing. He'd dealt with the town as he'd dealt with Alice that very first morning, making it clear that he wasn't going to tolerate any disrespect. Ted had never done that—but it wasn't fair, comparing Ted and Cole. Ted had been a good, decent man. Cole was—he was good, too. And decent. Yes, he'd used her years ago but that was then and this was now. And now, Cole was—he was—

He was the man she'd always wanted him to be, the man she could love…

She swung away, afraid he'd read the painful truth in her face, but he clasped her shoulders and turned her toward him.

"Faith? What's the matter?"

"Nothing," she said brightly. She looked up and smiled. "You've been wonderful for Peter."

He nodded. *How about for you?* he wanted to say. Have I been anything at all for you? But he knew the answer. She'd made it clear. She'd gone from despising him to tolerating him to being grateful to him for the kindness he'd shown the boy and suddenly, with gut-wrenching swiftness, he knew that wouldn't be enough. He didn't want her to be tolerant of him, dammit, or grateful. He wanted—he wanted…

"You said you had something to tell me," Faith said.

"Yeah." Cole took his hands from her shoulders. "Pete wants to join the Cub Scouts."

Faith blinked. "Really?"

"Turns out Billy Cullen—"

"The roller coaster expert," she said, and they both smiled.

"That's the kid. Turns out his old man is the scoutmaster and he's organized some kind of camping trip for the kids. Pete would like to go."

Her face fell. "He never said a word to me."

"Yeah." Cole smiled again. "Well, it's man stuff. You know. Anyway, I spoke with Billy's father—"

"Without discussing it with me first?"

"Don't get your back up, baby. Phil Cullen phoned a couple of days ago and I figured I'd check things out before I said anything to you."

Baby, he'd called her. She told herself she hated it when he did that…but she didn't. This time, the nickname hadn't sounded like a slur, it had sounded softly protective. Please,

Faith thought, oh, please, don't let this be happening to me all over again.

"The camp's in the mountains. It has a good reputation. So does Phil Cullen. Seems he takes the kids out every year."

She nodded. "I know. Peter mentioned it before. I asked him if he wanted to join the Pack but he said—"

"He said he didn't. Yeah, he told me. Well, I guess things have changed."

What he meant was, Peter wasn't an outcast anymore. Cole had done that for him.

"It looks like something he'd really enjoy, Faith. Cullen's a good guy, experienced with kids and with camping. They'll be gone for two weeks—"

"Two weeks!"

Cole smiled. "A lifetime, I know. But it'll be good for him. There'll be overnight hikes and cookouts. There are lots of activities at the camp and a doctor on the premises, and from what Cullen said, the food isn't half bad."

"Okay." She took a breath. "Peter can go."

Cole smiled. "Great. And the timing's perfect."

"What do you mean?"

He hesitated. She saw his eyes darken and instinctively, she knew that what was coming was going to change everything.

"You're—you're leaving," she said quietly.

He nodded. "I have to go to New York. There's no way out of it. There are some things on my calendar and…"

He went on talking. Faith nodded in what she thought might be the right places, she smiled politely, but she'd stopped listening. He was leaving, just as she'd hoped he would. He'd bent her to his will, given Peter some of the stability he'd promised, and now he was returning to his own world.

"…in a few months. I'll try, anyway, assuming nothing comes up…"

He'd try. In a few months, he'd try to fly down to see them. Not them. Peter. That was the only reason he'd forced her into this marriage. For Peter's sake. And thank goodness for that. She surely didn't want it any other way.

"Faith? You understand, don't you?"

"Of course." Somehow, she forced her lips to curve in a smile. "And don't worry about Peter."

Cole blinked. "Why would I? Pete'll do just fine."

"You're right. He'll miss you—"

"Miss me?"

"When you leave. But I'll explain that you couldn't possibly go on living here, with us. With him. And I'm sure he'll look forward to an occasional visit, whenever you can manage—"

She gasped as Cole clasped her shoulders. "You didn't hear a word I said."

"I did. You said you have to leave, that you'll try and visit us—visit Peter—in a few months—"

"No wonder you've been so obliging for the past half hour." Cole's mouth thinned. "'He's going,' you figured. You could afford to play the gracious lady and be pleasant."

Faith stared at him. "Aren't you? Going, I mean?"

"Oh, yeah, baby. I'm going." His eyes narrowed. "And so are you. That's what I meant about the timing being right. This way, Peter won't miss us while we're gone."

Was he speaking in English? Nothing he said made sense. "Gone where? Cole, I don't understand a word you're saying."

"That's because you were so busy trying not to jump up and down at the prospect of me being out of your life that you didn't listen." His hands tightened and he lifted her to her toes. "I'm going to New York. And you're going with me."

"Me? Going…? No! Our agreement never said—"

"You're my wife. You go where I go. I have a commitment in New York Friday night. Besides, it's time you got a look at your new home."

"My—my new home?" She knew she was parroting his words but she couldn't help it. What was he talking about?

"That's right, Faith. My home's in New York. That means our home will be there, too."

"No," she said again, her voice trembling. "That's impossible."

"The hell it is." His mouth turned down. "I know you

worship this—this pile of brick, but say goodbye to it, baby, because I'm selling it for the first offer I get.''

She could tell that he meant every word. Panic turned her blood to ice. She didn't want to go to New York. She was safe here, in the town she knew. In unknown territory, the rules would change.

"I'm not going. I'm not really your wife, no matter what you—"

"You're right. You aren't." He slid his hands up her throat and cupped her face. "But you will be, once we get to New York and I show you how worthless that damned prenup you're so proud of really is.''

"Don't,'' she said, but his mouth covered hers. He kissed her hard, his hands holding her captive, his mouth plundering hers until she began to tremble. "Don't,'' she said again, but it was a moan, a plea, and she lay her hands against his chest, caught his shirt in her fingers, lifted herself to him.

Cole groaned with pent-up desire. He swept his hands under her cotton T-shirt, cupped her breasts, felt the swift, tight beading of her nipples beneath the soft lace of her bra. The front closure tore apart in his hands and he spread his fingers over her naked flesh. Faith sobbed his name against his lips, dug her hands into his hair, dragged his face down to hers.

He could take her now. Put an end to all the sleepless nights. He could strip off her clothes, kiss every inch of her sweet body and make her his, forever, not because he'd forced her to sign an agreement but because she'd want to be his.

The enormity of the thought stunned him. He let go of her and she swayed unsteadily. Her face was pale but her cheeks were hot with color and when she opened her eyes and looked at him, it was through pupils so huge that all he could see of her irises was a thin rim of blue.

"Faith," he said. "Faith—"

He saw her hand lift and he knew what was coming but he did nothing to stop it. She slapped him, hard enough to make his head snap back.

"You son of a bitch," she whispered. "I hate you!"

She turned and raced up the stairs. He watched her go. Who

gave a damn if she hated him? He'd never meant more to her than a ticket out of a trailer park. And all she'd been to him was a hot, easy lay.

"Goddammit," he whispered.

Her heard her bedroom door slam. Slowly, he walked to the library. In the dark, he went to the cabinet where his old man had kept the booze. He wasn't much for hard liquor but he wanted something that would take the taste of ashes from his mouth.

A light came on inside the cabinet as he opened it. There were bottles lined up on the shelf. He reached for one marked Bourbon, not caring how long it might have stood there, poured an inch into a shot glass and downed the whiskey in one quick, searing gulp.

Faith hated him. So what? He really didn't give a damn.

And maybe, just maybe, if he told himself that often enough, he might even start to believe it.

CHAPTER ELEVEN

THEY flew to New York Friday afternoon, sitting in stiff silence side by side in the first class section of TransContinental Flight 937.

Faith wanted to be anywhere but on that plane. Still, at least they were alone. They could stop pretending everything was fine. They hadn't exchanged more than a handful of words in two days, except when Peter was around, and he was so excited about going to camp that it hadn't taken much effort to fool him.

The fiction ended when they boarded the plane. Faith accepted a magazine from the flight attendant without bothering to look at the cover. Cole opened a briefcase that he'd filled with documents from Ted's desk.

"I'm going to go through my brother's personal papers," he'd said last night. "Any objections?"

Why would she object? She and Ted had shared a house for nine years but they hadn't shared a life. In all the ways that mattered, they'd remained strangers. Still, as she watched Cole reach into the briefcase, she wondered if she should have gone through the papers first. Could there be anything in them that would give away Ted's secret, or hers? No, of course not. Ted had been cautious to the point of paranoia about what he'd called his other life, and she had Peter's birth certificate safely locked away.

Cole would be reading his brother's meticulous household records, nothing more.

Actually, he wasn't reading anything. He was staring out the window, the contents of the briefcase forgotten. Well, she wasn't doing much better. The magazine in her lap could have been printed in Sanskrit for all the attention she gave it. Anger still hummed in her blood and, she guessed, in his. She'd caught him looking at her with a light in his eyes that could only be fury.

What the hell did he have to be furious about?

Had he really expected her to bubble with joy when he announced that he was moving her from her home? Not that Liberty or Cameron House had ever actually felt like 'home', but that wasn't the point. Cole was taking over her life. First marriage, now the move to another state...and his threat about proving that the conditions of her prenuptial agreement were a travesty. The only way he could do that would be to take her by force and she couldn't imagine him doing that. Taking a woman who didn't want him. Carrying her to his bed. Subduing her struggles with kisses, with caresses, until her cries of protest became moans of desire...

A muffled sound slipped from her lips. Cole turned toward her.

"Did you say something?" he asked politely.

"No," she said, "I didn't." She opened the magazine and made a show of turning the pages until, at last, the plane touched down at La Guardia Airport.

A black Mercedes pulled to the curb as they exited the terminal. A young man in pressed blue jeans and a white shirt stepped out from behind the wheel, greeted Cole pleasantly and took her suitcase and his.

Don't bother packing anything but a toothbrush, Cole had told her curtly, you can find whatever you need in New York. She'd ignored him. Did he really think he'd buy her off with a shopping trip?

"This is John," Cole said. "He's the man you'll want if you need the car to take you anywhere. John, this is my wife."

John didn't so much as blink. "Mrs. Cameron," he said politely, "it's a pleasure to meet you."

Faith nodded but she didn't answer. Was she supposed to lie and say it was a pleasure to meet him, too? The only "pleasure" she could imagine would be Cole telling her he'd come to his senses and was setting her free.

Cole took her arm. She jerked it away, got into the Mercedes and scooted as far into the corner as she could. The car merged into a long line of vehicles and onto a traffic-clogged highway.

"This part of the city is called Queens," Cole said, after a few minutes.

Wonderful. Did he actually think she cared?

"Take the bridge please, John, so Mrs. Cameron can see the skyline."

The skyline. So what? Who hadn't see the New York skyline in the movies? And why would she give a damn? Tall buildings weren't going to make up for what was happening to her.

"Frankly," Faith said coldly, "I don't much care if I see the skyline or..." Her mouth dropped open. Just ahead, beyond a wide stretch of pewter-colored water, spires of concrete, glass and steel shouldered their way into the sky over the island of Manhattan. Faith forgot everything, her anger, her disdain, her determination to let nothing touch her. "Oh," she whispered, "oh, my!"

Cole could feel some of the tension seep from his muscles. Not that he cared whether or not his wife liked his city... Okay. Yeah, he did. It had nothing to do with how he felt about the place, that he'd come to love the energy of it, the bustle of its streets and the tranquility of its parks, it was just that—it was just that...

Maybe he did want her to like New York. To feel what he felt. From the awed expression on her face, she just might.

"It's beautiful," she said.

He nodded. "I remember the first time I saw that view." A smile softened his voice. "I couldn't decide whether I was excited or scared stiff."

Faith raised an eyebrow. "The great Cole Cameron, scared?"

Her ready disdain angered him. What could she possibly know about how far he'd traveled to get where he was? Not in miles, though he'd put on lots of those. In sweat. In hard work. In risks taken with only the hope of a better future on the distant horizon.

"Sorry," he said coldly. "I didn't mean to bore you."

Faith looked at him. He was staring straight ahead, his profile stern and implacable, but some quality in his voice made her regret her words.

"You didn't," she said quickly. "I just...it's hard to imagine you afraid of anything."

A long moment went by. Then his expression eased, if only a little. "Maybe scared is the wrong word. Intimidated. That's what I was." He laughed. "Intimidated, all the way down to my toes. I guess I'd never pictured a place bigger than Atlanta or Corpus Christi."

"Corpus Christi?"

"Yeah. That's where I went after—after I left Liberty."

"Ah. After you left Liberty." She spoke politely. "And how long had you planned that?"

Cole heaved a sigh. So much for the temporary thaw. "I never had a plan."

"Really?" she said, even more politely. "You could have fooled me."

Cole swung toward her. "You think you know me," he said coldly. "But I promise you, Faith, you don't."

No. No, she didn't. And she didn't want to. She'd been foolish, letting him lead her into this conversational dance. Did he think she'd be easier to deal with if she knew what he'd been doing for the past nine years? She didn't care where he'd been or why he'd gone there, didn't care if he loved New York or Timbuktu.

The Mercedes turned onto Fifth Avenue. She recognized it the same way she had the skyline. Who wouldn't find those elegant apartment buildings familiar, or the green of Central Park? So what? Did he think he could impress her with his wealth?

The driver pulled to the curb. A uniformed doorman opened the door to the car just as Cole reached for the handle.

"Mr. Cameron, sir. It's good to have you back."

"Otto. Thank you. It's good to be back." Cole stepped onto the sidewalk and offered her his hand. Faith made a point of looking at it before brushing past him on her own. Cole's eyes glittered dangerously. She felt a shiver of apprehension, as if she were five years old again, playing with a matchbook she'd found in the trailer. "This is my wife," he said. His hand closed on her elbow, hard enough so she knew it would be a mistake to try and pull away. "She's quite an independent-minded woman but I'm sure she'll permit you to find her a taxi when she needs one."

Otto smiled pleasantly. "Hello, Mrs. Cameron. It'll be a pleasure to serve you."

Faith smiled politely, just as she smiled at the concierge seated behind an antique desk in the lobby. Cole led her to the elevator and inserted a key opposite a number on the panel. The doors whooshed closed and the car began a smooth ascent. Smooth or not, her stomach still dropped. This is my new life, she kept thinking, the life I'm expected to lead with a stranger.

The elevator stopped and the doors opened on an endless expanse of marble. A man dressed in a black suit came toward them, smiling pleasantly.

"Welcome home, Mr. Cameron."

"Thank you, Dobbs." Cole drew Faith forward. "Dobbs, this is my wife. Please have a key made for her as soon as possible."

"Certainly, sir."

A key. Of course. This was some kind of upstairs lobby...but where were the doors to the other apartments?

"We're on the penthouse level," Cole said quietly. Had she spoken out loud or was he as good at reading minds as he was at turning all her expectations upside down? "You'll need the key for the elevator. It opens directly into the entry foyer."

"Shall I take your things up now, sir?"

"Thank you, Dobbs. That can wait until later. Just now, I think Mrs. Cameron and I would like some coffee." Cole's hand tightened on Faith's elbow. "Faith?"

She looked up at him, her eyes dark with bewilderment. He thought about all the changes he was making in her life and felt a stir of compassion. His hand slid down her arm, his fingers twined in hers. Never mind the coffee. She needed to rest for a little while. He'd take his wife upstairs, take her in his arms, lie down with her on the bed—their bed—and she could put her head on his shoulder, close her eyes and maybe she'd realize this wasn't the end of the world.

It could be a new beginning for them both.

"Faith," he said gently. "Let me show you to our room."

Our room? *Our* room? The two simple words jolted her into reality. Faith twisted her hand free of Cole's.

"You can show me to *my* room," she said, "not to *our* room. I've no intention of—"

"Up you go," Cole said briskly, and swung her into his arms.

Caught by surprise, she gasped and looped her arms around his neck but by the time he'd carried her through the foyer and up a curving staircase, she'd recovered her senses.

"Damn you," she said, "put me down!"

Cole marched into a room, shouldered the door shut and dumped her on her feet. His face was white with anger.

"Do not," he growled, "ever do that to me again!"

"I beg your pardon?"

"You'd better beg my pardon. You will not speak to me that way in front of people. You are my wife, and I expect you to behave like it."

"Why?" Faith slapped her hands on her hips. "Will it make your audience think less of you if I don't?"

"Get this through your head, baby. I've taken as much of your antics as I'm going to take." Cole took a step toward her. "You got that?"

"Oh, I've got it. You expect me to kowtow like the rest of your entourage."

"You are my wife. I expect a show of respect."

"Just as long as you understand it's only a show."

Cole stripped off his jacket and his tie and tossed them on a chair. "I'm warning you," he said through his teeth. "Don't push me. I've had just about enough."

"You've had enough?" Faith flung her purse after his jacket and tie. "You uproot me from my life, take me to this— this place where people do everything but prostrate themselves when they see you coming—"

"They do no such thing!"

"Oh, give me a break. Of course they do." Her words took on a tone that made him think of oil oozing from the ground. "'How are you, sir?' 'Welcome home, sir.' 'It's a pleasure to serve you, sir.'"

"Would you prefer they boo and hiss at the sight of me?"

She looked at him. He was right. There was nothing wrong with the way anybody had greeted him. His driver, the doorman, the butler—they'd been polite, not obsequious. *He* had been polite to them in turn. He'd been polite to everyone but her. He only snapped orders at her.

"You're the one who needs lessons in courtesy," Cole said sharply. "Did you once think of responding properly to John or Otto or anybody else? Did you think of extending your hand and saying you were pleased to meet them?"

"I'm not pleased. I don't want to meet your servants."

"Dammit, Faith, they are not my servants. They're my employees."

"There's a difference?"

"There sure as hell is." Cole stalked across the room as he opened his shirt. A button popped under his angry touch and dropped to the carpet. "Servants take orders. They say 'Yes, sir.' 'No, sir.' 'Right away, sir,' and I'll be damned if I'd ever expect a man or woman to do any of that crap for me." The furious rush of words stopped. In the sudden silence, Faith could hear the ragged sound of his breathing. "I don't have servants," he said tightly. "I have people who work for me. I pay them well. I respect them and they respect me. I would never dream of humiliating them. And I will not tolerate having you humiliate them *or* me. Is that clear?"

Faith stared at this stranger who was her husband. Nothing was clear. The more time they spent together, the less she understood him, but he was right and she knew it. He hadn't treated anyone badly. She had. And she had no idea why.

"Is it?" he demanded.

He was glowering at her, lines of anger etched into his face. Her throat tightened. She made him angry all the time. She hadn't, years ago. Back then, he'd always smiled when he saw her. *Faith,* he'd say, in a way that turned her name into a caress, *Faith, baby,* and her heart would turn over with the rightness of it.

"I didn't..." She hesitated. "I didn't mean to treat anyone badly," she said quietly. Her head came up. "I know it's not their fault that—all of this is happening."

"You don't want to live here." Cole spoke stiffly, as if each word were difficult to form. "I know that. But *I* live here. I have offices here." He let out a slow breath. "This is my home."

But it wasn't hers, she almost said...except, had she ever really thought of a place as "home"? She'd certainly never felt that way about the trailer, when she was growing up, or about Cameron House. The only place that had ever felt remotely like home had been Cole's arms, but look what had come of those foolish daydreams.

Her spine stiffened. "And you expect me to make the best of it."

His mouth thinned. "Yes."

"In that case, I want separate bedrooms, the way it was at Cameron House."

"To hell with Cameron House," he roared. Faith jerked back in shock. What was wrong with him? Anger boiled in his blood and for what reason? Because his wife wasn't singing hosannas over the city he loved or the life he'd carved for himself? Because she didn't see he could give her things no man had ever given her?

Was he really that crazy? Did it matter?

Yes, he thought furiously, yes, it did, and he grabbed her shoulders and yanked her to her toes.

"You're my wife and you're damned well going to begin behaving as if you are! Forget Cameron House. Forget my brother. This is your life, Faith, starting right now. You're going to share this room. This bed. You're going to treat me like a husband, and don't waste your breath telling me about that damn-fool piece of paper I signed because I'm not interested. Have you got that?" He looked down into her eyes, into her white face and he cursed, bent his head and kissed her.

She reacted instantly, twisting against his hands, trying to tear free and when he slid his hands up, cupped her face and held her prisoner to his passion, she sank her teeth into his bottom lip. Cole said something under his breath, tunneled his fingers into her hair and kissed her again, his mouth relentless, his grip remorseless, and suddenly Faith sobbed and opened her mouth to his. Cole gathered her closer against him and she wound her arms tightly around his neck, lifting herself to him, melding her body to his.

The tap at the door was like a clap of thunder. They sprang apart and stared at each other, both of them breathing hard.

"Yes?" Cole said roughly, his eyes never leaving her face.

"Your coffee, sir."

A muscled knotted in Cole's jaw. "Just—just leave the tray in the hall, thank you, Dobbs."

"Yes, sir."

They went on staring at each other. Finally, Faith put a hand to her flushed face. "I don't know what you want from me," she whispered shakily.

He didn't, either. There were times he wanted to hurt her but there were other times when he wanted to cradle her in his arms, hold her against his heart...

He took a step back. "We have a dinner engagement." His voice was calm. "And you have less than an hour to get yourself ready for it."

"I don't want—"

"This is your bathroom." He opened a door. Beyond it gleamed black tile, silver faucets and mirrored walls. "Go through it and you'll be in your dressing room. You'll find everything you need, I think. Cosmetics, toiletries, clothes..."

Faith drew herself up. "I don't use other women's left-overs."

"Everything is new, right down to the soaps." He looked at her, smiled politely. "It's amazing, what a man can arrange through the services of a personal shopper. Now..." He glanced at his watch. "Now, we're down to fifty minutes. Since I have no idea how long it takes you to transform yourself into a vision suitable for an evening out, I suggest you get started.''

''I wouldn't begin to know how to transform myself into a vision.''

''If you're fishing for compliments, forget it. I'm not about to tell you that you're always beautiful because you already know it.''

Her head jerked up. She stared at him. ''What?''

Cole walked toward her, eyes cool, mouth curved in what was almost a smile, every step filled with determination. ''I said, you're beautiful. Too beautiful for a man ever to forget.'' Something flickered in his eyes as he reached for her and drew her to him. ''I never forgot anything,'' he said softly.

''Be careful or I'll bite you again.'' She tossed back her hair and hoped he couldn't see the pulse racing in her throat. ''How would you explain fang marks to your friends?''

''Some of the men would see it as a badge of honor.'' He lifted one hand, let it take a slow path over her mouth. ''They'd figure it meant you can't control yourself when I'm around.''

''You wish,'' she said, and tried not to smile.

He looked at her mouth, then into her eyes. ''What I wish is that I could pass on this dinner,'' he said softly. ''But it's for charity and I said I'd be there.''

''I didn't,'' she said lightly.

''We're married, Faith.'' He tipped her head up. She held her breath, waiting, reading his eyes, knowing what he would do, telling herself it wasn't what she wanted, but when he lowered his head to hers, touched his mouth to hers, she sighed. ''Where I go,'' he said, ''you go.''

''But not to bed,'' she whispered.

God, he thought, God, how he wanted her. Her protest held no meaning. She was still denying the truth, but only with words. Her body, her compliant body, her parted lips, her shining eyes gave a different message. It took every bit of willpower he possessed to let go of her.

''Get dressed,'' he said gently. ''Put on something long. The dinner is black tie.''

"I don't own anything long."

"Yes, baby, you do. Check out the dressing room. I didn't know what you'd want so... I mean, I told that personal shopper how I thought you'd look in some colors, some different kinds of things..." He took a deep breath. "Faith. Go find something you like and put it on."

Where was she?

Cole paced the bedroom and glowered at his watch. Seven forty-four. Exactly two minutes had passed since the last time he'd checked. Wasn't she ready yet?

He'd knocked on her dressing room door a little while ago. "Faith?" he'd called. "Are you ready?"

"Five more minutes," she'd said.

And he'd said he hoped so because it was getting late—which wasn't exactly true. The dinner invitation read eight-thirty, meaning nobody would dare arrive before eight forty-five, nine if they wanted to be safely fashionable. Besides, the party was taking place in a town house just a couple of blocks away. So it wasn't getting late. They had plenty of time. The trouble was, he was going crazy out here.

Tonight, he was going to present his wife to the world.

Cole frowned and dug his hands into the pockets of his trousers. Well, no. This wasn't exactly the world. These people weren't even his friends. They were nice enough, most of them, but they were acquaintances, that was all.

Still, this was The Night. He was about to introduce Faith as his wife. Once upon a time, a lifetime ago, that had been what he'd dreamed of doing. Of walking up to people with her beside him and saying, "This is my wife. The woman I love."

His frown deepened. He paced across the floor again.

Things had changed. He wasn't an embittered kid. She wasn't an innocent girl—if that was a word that had ever applied to Faith. They were adults and she had belonged to another man. To his brother. And it was time to put all that behind them. For Peter's sake, not for any other reason. For the boy—

"Cole?"

He turned around. His wife stood in the center of the room. Her hair was drawn back from her face, falling in a tumble of golden waves over her shoulders. Her eyes were the color of the Georgia sky on a midsummer morning and by some minor miracle, she was wearing the only gown he'd actually selected from a stack of faxes the personal shopper had sent him because it was so perfect for her, because he'd been able to shut his eyes and see Faith, his Faith, wearing that sweep of red silk.

He went to her. She watched him approach, her expression solemn.

"Faith," he said softly, and gathered her into his arms. He waited for her to object. Instead, she looked at him as if she'd never seen him before. He held his breath, waiting, and then she whispered his name and he kissed her, and she kissed him back with such tenderness that he could feel his heart fill.

In that moment, Cole knew the truth. The past didn't matter. Her motives didn't matter.

He had never stopped loving her.

Something had changed.

Faith stared the length of the table at the man who was her husband. The man to her right was telling her something about the new van Gogh exhibit at the Met and she wanted to pay attention because she'd seen pictures of some of van Gogh's paintings and they'd always moved her, really, they had.

But nothing moved her like the sight of her husband. And how could that be? She hated Cole...didn't she?

Maybe it was the way he looked that made for the change. It was hard to hate a man who was so handsome. Gorgeous, really, especially in his tux. She liked the way his hair fell over his forehead, the way he kept pushing it back with his hand. He'd done that years ago, the exact same way. His hair had been a little longer then, maybe a little lighter...

What a beautiful man he was.

She wished she could tell him that but it wasn't a thing you could say to a man. *Hi, and oh, by the way, did you know you're beautiful?* She could just imagine his reaction. He'd look at her as if she were crazy, or he'd laugh and tell her a guy couldn't be beautiful... Except, he was. Beautiful. And he was hers. He was her husband.

Faith picked up her wineglass and took a sip. The Chardonnay was cool on her tongue, which was good. She'd felt warm all evening. Nobody else seemed to be. Some of the women, in fact, had joked about feeling chilly but she was warm. Sometimes, she even felt hot. Like now, when Cole— when her husband—turned away from the woman seated to his left and looked the length of the table at her.

She could read the message in his eyes. *Faith. You're my wife. And I want you.*

The glass trembled in her hand as she sipped the wine again. Yes, something had changed. One minute, she'd been burning with anger. The next—the next, she'd looked at the man she'd once loved and she'd known—she'd known—

The glass slipped from her suddenly nerveless fingers and splintered on the table. Conversation ceased as pale gold liquid spread across the white damask. Mortified, she dabbed at the puddle with her napkin.

"I'm sorry," she said, and found every eye on her. "I'm terribly sorry."

"That's quite all right," their hostess said graciously, as a maid hurried toward Faith. "My husband always said these glasses aren't properly balanced. I just hope you didn't spoil that lovely gown."

"No," Faith said, her voice shaking, "I didn't. But I've broken the glass—"

"Faith." She looked up. Cole was standing beside her. "Baby," he said, so gently that she felt tears prick her eyes. He pulled back her chair and drew her up beside him, his arm curving protectively around her waist. He smiled at her, then at their hostess. "It's been a wonderful evening," he said, "but my wife is exhausted."

My wife, Faith thought, *my wife.*

"It's been a long day for her. For the both of us. We should have stayed home this evening, but—"

"But I wanted to meet you," Faith said softly. "I wanted to meet all my husband's friends."

She looked up at Cole and let him see the truth glowing in her eyes, and to delighted murmurs and a smattering of applause, he swept her into his arms and carried her from the room.

"But what will they think?" Faith whispered, as John drove them home.

"They'll think I'm the luckiest man in the world," Cole said gruffly. She was still in his arms—he'd refused to put her down. The privacy panel was up, the windows were opaque. No one could see them or hear them but he hadn't touched her. Not yet. Nothing but the lightest of kisses, the softest brush of his hand against her cheek. Wait, he told himself, wait until we're alone, until I can do this right.

He told himself that all the way up to the penthouse, thought it as he carried Faith up the curving staircase and into the dark bedroom. Wait. Go slowly. Don't hurry the moment you've waited for, for so long.

But when the door swung shut, Faith sighed his name, framed his face in her hands and drew his head down to hers. She kissed him, her mouth soft, her taste sweet, and he was lost.

"Faith," he said, and he kissed her throat. "Faith..."

"Make love to me," she whispered. "Make love to me. Please."

Cole's fingers shook as he unzipped her gown. Beneath it, she wore a black silk camisole, panties, a garter belt and black hose. He kissed her nipples through the sheer silk, cupped her wet warmth, groaned when she trembled. He wanted to tell her she was beautiful, far more wonderful than in all his remembrances, but she was undoing his tie, his studs; she was easing his jacket off. She was opening his belt, his fly...

With a growl of need he pushed her hands away, finished undressing them both, lifted her in his arms again and carried her to the bed.

"I wanted to make this last," he said roughly. "But I can't, baby. I need you. I've always needed you."

"Cole," Faith said, and held up her arms, "now. Oh, now..."

He knelt between her thighs. "I love you, Faith," he said, and then he entered her on one long, deep thrust. She arched toward him, cried out his name, and the world shattered into a million fiery bits of light.

CHAPTER TWELVE

IT WAS as if the years had slipped away.

Lying in Cole's arms, feeling his body hard and warm against hers, Faith could almost believe she was seventeen again and that life was a bright ribbon stretching ahead.

How could she have thought that she wasn't still in love with this man? She turned her face until her lips were against his shoulder. She had never forgotten the taste of him or his scent, or how she felt when he held her this way. Safe. Protected.

Loved.

I love you, Faith. That was what he'd said, just as he had that night so many years ago. And even if he hadn't meant it then, he had to mean it now. He wasn't a boy anymore, he was a man. He had married her for the wrong reasons but those words, those three wonderful words, had conviction now, and meaning. They had to because if they didn't, if they didn't...

"Baby?" Cole leaned on his elbow and gently stroked her hair back from her temple. "Are you all right?"

"Oh, yes." Faith raised her hand, cupped his jaw, felt the faint stubble of his beard abrade her soft flesh as he clasped her hand and brought it to his mouth. She caught her breath, shivered with pleasure as he took a love bite from the pad of flesh just below her thumb. "I'm fine."

"I didn't mean to go so fast." Cole gathered her against him, slid one hand slowly up and down her back. "It's just that I wanted you so badly... It's been so long, baby. Sometimes it feels as if a century's passed since the night of the prom." He kissed her mouth gently. "I've never forgotten that night, Faith. I couldn't believe I'd finally made you mine."

165

The softly-spoken words sent a swift, sharp pain through her heart. *Then, why did you leave me?* she thought, but she didn't ask the question. This wasn't the time to hear the answer.

She smiled and toyed with the lock of hair that had fallen over his forehead. "It was a wonderful night. *You* were wonderful."

Cole grinned. "Well, if you insist…"

Faith laughed softly. "My modest hero."

His smile faded. "I'm no hero, sweetheart. If I were, I wouldn't have left you." He rolled her onto her back. "We need to talk about what happened, Faith."

"No," she said quickly. Oh, no. They couldn't. Not now. She knew he was right, that the only way to build a future was to face the past, but there were so many painful secrets to divulge, the truth about Peter and, inevitably, about Ted… The miracle of their rediscovered love was too new. Too fragile. Surely, things that had been hidden for so long could wait for morning. Faith clasped her husband's face and kissed him. "I don't want to talk," she whispered. "Not tonight."

"You're right. Tonight is special."

She smiled. "Yes."

"When I think of all the time we've been apart…" Cole stopped in midsentence. This was all that mattered, that she was his again, that she would always be his. "We have our whole lives ahead of us, Faith," he said softly. "I'm never going to lose you again."

He gave her a slow, deep kiss, then drew back just enough so he could see her face. "First thing tomorrow morning, I'm going to call my attorney."

She looked puzzled. "What for?"

Cole smiled. "I'm going to tell him that he can tear up that prenup you signed."

"You don't have to do that, Cole. I'm not—I wouldn't want anything of yours if—if something went wrong between—"

He silenced her with another kiss. "Nothing will go wrong," he said softly. "I promise you that. This marriage is forever." His smile tilted. "You and I are going to spend the next hundred years together."

She laughed. "I hope so."

"Me, too." Cole cupped her face. "I don't want that piece of paper between us, baby. I made you sign it before I was ready to admit the truth, that I love you, that I've always loved you despite…" He cleared his throat. "We're going to put the past behind us, and we're going to start by tearing up that prenup." He bent his head, kissed her throat. "What's fair is fair, Mrs. Cameron. After all, we've already disposed of the terms of yours."

She smiled and put her arms around him. "I noticed."

"What else did you notice?" For instance…" Her breath hitched as he cupped her breast. "Did you notice," he said, his voice suddenly thick, "what happens to your nipple when I brush my thumb over it, like this?"

"Cole." She shut her eyes, then opened them again. "Yes. I—I noticed. I…"

"Or when I do this?" he whispered, kissing her breasts, closing his teeth lightly around first one pearled tip and then the other.

A soft moan rose from her throat. She shifted her weight, her body suddenly hot and lithe against his, and Cole felt himself turning to stone.

"You have beautiful breasts, sweetheart. Did I tell ever tell you that?"

"Tell me now," she said huskily, her voice breaking as he bent his head to her again, took her eager flesh into his mouth.

Cole lifted his head. His eyes were almost black with desire. "Not until you say the words I've waited a lifetime to hear," he murmured.

Faith could feel her heart swell with love. "I love you," she said softly. "I love you, Cole, I love—"

She cried out as he put his hand between her thighs and found the soft, secret portal of her womanhood.

"Faith," he said, and opened her to him.

And after that, for a very long time, nothing else mattered.

*   *   *

Cole jerked awake, torn from sleep by a bad dream.

Really bad, he thought, and shuddered. Sweat dampened his skin, even though the room was cool. It was amazing, what a nightmare could do. What in hell had he dreamed? Something about Faith. And Ted.

The images were fading. He shook them off. Bad dreams about his wife and his brother shouldn't be on his mind now. The last thing he wanted was to think about stuff like that tonight. He didn't want to think about it any night. All of that was history. The present, and the future, were right here in the curve of his arm.

He turned his head, pressed a soft kiss into Faith's silky hair. She sighed, murmured something in her sleep and flung an arm across his chest. Cole smiled, drew her closer against him and shut his eyes, but after a little while he opened them and glanced at the lighted bedside clock.

Was it really just a few minutes after two? They'd been asleep for only a couple of hours but he felt energized.

Love could do that for a man, he thought, and kissed his wife's forehead.

The digital numbers on the clock's face blinked. Two-ten. Two-fifteen. Cole sighed and carefully eased his arm from beneath Faith's shoulders. She rolled onto her belly. He thought about waking her, kissing his way down her body from the sweet-scented nape of her neck to that little dimple at the base of her spine. He knew what would happen, that she would turn to him even before she was fully awake, sigh his name, reach for him and draw him deep, deep inside her...

He was hard as a rock.

No. He wasn't going to wake Faith. She had to be exhausted. They'd made love again and again, his need for her unending, hers for him every bit as intense, though she'd winced the last time he'd entered her.

"Baby?" he'd said softly. "Am I hurting you?"

"No," she'd whispered, "oh, no. Don't stop. Don't..."

And she'd moved, put her hand between them and touched him and he couldn't have stopped, not for anything, not until her body convulsed around his.

"Damn," Cole whispered, and rose from the bed.

Let Faith sleep. He'd worn her out. No matter what she said, she'd been tender that last time, tender and still so tight that he'd almost been able to forget she'd spent her nights in another man's arms for the past nine years...

Except, she hadn't. Wasn't that what Jergen had told him? That Faith had kept Ted out of her bed? That Ted had to seek solace with a woman in Atlanta?

Cole frowned. What was the matter with him? The last thing he wanted to think about tonight was his brother's sexual relationship with Faith.

He made his way through the darkened bedroom to his dressing room, pulled on a pair of sweatpants and went down the stairs to his study. That kind of thinking was bad news. Whatever had gone on between Faith and Ted had been their business. Besides, Jergen's stories were probably exaggerated. Everybody in town, the lawyer included, would have judged Faith Davenport harshly, maybe even made up the facts to suit their own vivid imaginations.

Faith had told him that she'd loved Ted.

He believed her.

Cole sat down at his desk and turned on the light. He reached for the briefcase he'd brought back from Liberty. It was still crammed with Ted's papers, nothing important, from the fast look he'd taken at the top two or three things. Still, the papers had to be gone through before he could dispose of them. He'd already turned up a couple of bills that needed to be paid.

Yeah, that would make the hours pass, he thought as he dumped the contents of the briefcase on his desk. Go through the papers, save the few that mattered, throw out the rest. Middle of the night thoughts could be bleak. Why waste time letting them prey on his mind? Yes, Faith had married Ted. And yes, she'd borne his child. So, okay. Imagining her in his brother's arms was lousy. Even thinking about her body, rounded and full with Ted's baby...

"Hell," he said into the silence. Enough of that. He began rifling through the papers.

It was dull stuff. A plumbing bill. An estimate for a new roof. A forgotten shopping list and a note from the gardener, suggesting he move the rosebushes. This detritus was all that remained of Ted. Bills, estimates, shopping lists...

What in hell was that? Cole reached into the wastebasket, plucked out a piece of paper he'd tossed in automatically, before his brain had fully registered the contents.

Teddy, my own...

Cole frowned. This wasn't Faith's handwriting.

Teddy, my own. I miss you terribly. I hate living like this, seeing you only once a month and sharing stolen moments...

Cole's gaze dropped to the bottom of the page. *Jessie,* it said, in a sinuous, feminine hand.

He stopped reading, looked up blindly and stared at the wall. Ted had spent one week a month in Atlanta, Jergen had said. He'd had a woman there.

So what?

Cole crumpled the note in his fist, tossed it into the basket and began rapidly thumbing through the papers. The past was dead, wasn't that what he'd told himself? He wasn't going to sit in judgment on Ted, or on a woman named Jessie...or on Faith, who'd said she'd loved his brother, that Jergen's accusations were a lie...

His breath caught. Another note, in the same handwriting and with that same signature. Don't read it, he told himself, dammit, don't.

It would have been easier to have told himself to stop breathing.

...so happy. Everyone is entitled to happiness, Teddy, and to love. I adore you and I know you feel the same way but here we are, kept apart by your damned determination to honor an obligation to a marriage that's always been a sham...

Cole's mouth hardened. He gave up all pretence of looking at receipts or anything else. Were there other notes from Jessie? He leaned over the stack of papers, went through them deliberately—and found more.

...ever occurred to you that she used you? I know you don't want to hear this, Teddy, because you feel responsible for the child, but I beg you to consider what I'm saying....

...doesn't share your life, doesn't want to know anything about the real person inside you. How can you exist that way? How can you live a lie?

Cole's eyes burned with unshed tears. Ted's secret life was spread before him, the emptiness of it, the lack of love. He didn't want to read any more, didn't want to know any more...

And then he found an envelope, already addressed in his brother's hand. It had never been sealed or mailed. Slowly, Cole withdrew a single sheet of paper and unfolded it.

...asked me if there's any affection between Faith and me. I know what you're thinking, Jess, that sometimes, even in a situation like ours, a man can be torn in two directions. I promise you, that's not the way it is. The truth is that I wish it were. How much simpler my life would be if your accusations were true. If Faith loved me. If she shared my bed. But she doesn't. Does it really matter how she got pregnant? She did, that's all. And I married her. I have an obligation to her, Jess. I will, until Peter is grown. I had to do the right thing....

The letter slipped from Cole's fingers. He buried his head in his hands. Ted, he thought, oh, Ted. Marrying a woman and not even knowing how she'd gotten herself pregnant. Doing it because it was the right thing to do. Loving her, wanting her to love him and knowing she didn't. Being kept out of her bed so that you eventually got so lonely you sought love elsewhere...

"Cole?"

Cole shot to his feet. His wife—his scheming, heartless wife—stood just inside the doorway. She was wearing something he'd bought her, a pale blue silk robe that hung open just enough to show the soft curves of her breasts, the flatness of her belly. Her hair hung to her shoulders in a mass of golden curls, her mouth was gently swollen from his kisses. She looked beautiful and as innocent as the day he'd first met her...

And he had to curl his hands into fists to keep from going to her and wrapping his fingers around her throat.

"Couldn't you sleep?" She came toward him, a beautiful witch who'd destroyed his brother's life and come within a heartbeat of doing the same thing to his. "I woke up and you were gone." She lay her hands against his naked chest, tipped her face up to him and smiled. "Come back to bed, darling."

Darling. Just a little while ago, he'd have given his soul to hear that word on her lips. Now he knew it for what it was, a lie like all her others, meant to chain everything that he was to her.

"Cole?" Her smile dimmed. "What's the matter?"

"Why should anything be the matter?"

"I don't know. You just—you look so strange..."

"You don't." He clasped her wrists, his fingers like manacles around them. "You look the same as you always do, Faith. Beautiful, innocent and guileless. So guileless."

"Cole." Her tongue snaked out, moistened her lips. She gave a quick little laugh. "You're scaring me."

"Am I?" He smiled thinly, tightened his grasp on her wrists. "I'll bet you weren't afraid of my brother."

"Of course not. Why would I have been afraid of Ted?" She tried to tug her hands free. "Cole, let go."

"He had to do the right thing," he said roughly. She winced; he knew his fingers must be biting into her wrists but he didn't give a damn. "Was that his idea, Faith? Or is that what you told him?"

"Told who?" She grimaced. "You're hurting me."

"No, baby. Hurting people is your thing, not mine."

"Dammit, what is this?"

"What a pathetic pair the Cameron brothers were, Faith. Both of us, drooling over you and almost tripping over our feet in our desperate rush to do the right thing."

Her face whitened. "What are you talking about?"

He jerked his head toward the desk. "I've been going through my brother's papers."

"Ted's..." She looked at the desk, then at him. "And—and what did you find?"

He smiled tightly. "Oh, baby," he said softly, "you should see those eyes of yours. Big and beautiful—and terrified." He tugged her closer, ignoring the little cry she made. "I found it all, Faith, everything I needed to know the truth."

"The truth..."

She stared at him in horror. Possibilities tumbled through her mind. What had he found? A copy of Peter's birth certificate that Ted hadn't mentioned? A picture of Ted and—and someone else? She'd stumbled across a photo, once, innocent enough, of Ted and a man with their arms around each other's shoulders, but Ted had blushed and apologized and said it would never happen again. Would Cole know what he was looking at, even if he discovered such a picture?

"What truth?" she whispered.

"Come on, baby. The act is finished. I can almost see those wheels turning. What lie are you gonna come up with, now?"

Peter, she thought frantically, this had to be about Peter. Otherwise, why would Cole be looking at her with such hatred in his eyes?

"All right." She hesitated, trying to find a way to explain things to him. How desperate she'd been. How alone. "I swear, I was going to tell you. I just—I wanted to wait until the morning."

"Of course you did," Cole said silkily. "Morning's when the payoff was due. When I was going to phone my lawyer and tell him to rip up the prenup."

She jerked back as if he'd struck her. "How can you think that of me? I don't want your money. I told you that. I never wanted—"

"It must have been rough, thinking you'd landed a Cameron and then having him slip out of your greedy little fingers at the last minute."

Faith blinked. "What?"

"There you were, all ready for the big payoff."

"I don't understand—"

"Sure you do." Cole smiled. "You wanted a Cameron. Well hell, Faith, I wanted the trailer park queen."

Her face went white. "No. You said—you said you loved me..."

"A kid that age will say anything to get into a girl's pants." The pain in her eyes filled him with pleasure. It was long past time someone returned the favor, showed Faith Davenport what it was like to see your dreams ripped in pieces. "I'd been planning to leave Liberty for months." That lie came easily, too. "The morning after the prom seemed just right. The only thing was, I'd figured I'd have to work a little bit harder to get between your legs. Sort of a farewell present from you to me, you know?"

Faith had stopped struggling to free her hands. She stood very still, tears spilling from her eyes.

"Last night," she whispered, "last night you said—you said you loved me..."

"Sure. Can you think of an easier way to take that stupid prenup of yours and stuff it down your throat?" He grinned. "It's called revenge, Faith. Revenge for me, for my brother, for the woman who managed to make my brother happy despite you."

"The woman who..." Faith stared at him. "The woman who...?" A bubble of laughter burst from her throat.

"I'm glad you think this is funny," Cole growled. "You won't be laughing when you find yourself out on your butt, with my lawyers suing you for custody of my brother's son. I'm not going to dissolve this marriage, baby. You are." He looked at her in disgust, reached for the intercom on his desk and pressed a button. "I don't know why I'm wasting my time talking to you. I'll wake Dobbs. He'll take you to the airport. I want you out of my sight, out of my home...out of Peter's life."

Faith stared at him, terrified of what she heard in his voice. "You can't. The attorney said so. He said no court would—"

"If he's right, I'll find another way." Cole's eyes narrowed. "The bottom line is that you're not going to raise my brother's son."

"Sir?" Dobbs said, over the intercom.

"Take Mrs. Cameron to the airport," Cole said brusquely.

"Now, sir?"

"Now."

He swung away and began stuffing Ted's papers back into the briefcase. When he looked up again, Faith was gone.

CHAPTER THIRTEEN

FAITH glanced at her watch as she stood in the tiny kitchen of her Atlanta apartment and gulped down the last of her morning coffee.

It was almost nine o'clock. If she didn't hurry, she'd be late. This was her fourth interview of the week but she had a good feeling about it. She might not have the credentials the store wanted—she'd never sold anything in her life—but at least she knew something about children's clothing.

How quickly they grew out of it, for instance.

She sighed as she plucked Peter's shirt from the back of a chair. He was shooting up like a weed. By the time school started next month, he'd need new pants and new shoes. She just had to find work before then. So far, she'd charged everything on her credit card, and the fifteen hundred dollars she'd needed to pay the first two months rent on this apartment had wiped out her checking account.

She was flat broke. If she didn't get a job soon…

There was no point in thinking about 'soon,' she told herself firmly. One day at a time. That was all she could handle without panicking. As it was, she'd been lucky to find this place. It was only two furnished room with a small kitchen and an even smaller bathroom, but it was clean and the neighborhood was worn-looking but safe. Peter had made friends with the twins who lived down the hall. He seemed happy enough—she suspected he saw their new life as an adventure—though he kept asking when he was going to see Cole again.

Faith had tried to be as honest as she could.

She'd driven to the Scout camp as soon as she'd returned from New York. Peter had fussed a little when she told him she was taking him home.

176

"I'm having a good time, Mom," he'd said. "Do I have to leave?"

"Yes," she'd said firmly.

He'd been even more puzzled when they reached Cameron House and he saw the cartons she'd picked up at the supermarket.

"Here," she'd said, with a smile she hoped might fool him. "Take a box, Peter, and start packing your toys."

"Why?" her son had asked. "Where are we going?"

"Peter. We don't have much time. Take a box upstairs and—"

"Where's Cole? Isn't he going with us? He said he was gonna be my new father."

Faith had spewed out a string of platitudes and feel-good white lies. Peter hadn't believed any of them. Eventually, she'd taken him on her lap and told him that things didn't always work out the way grown-ups expected.

Her son's face had fallen. "You mean, we're gonna get a divorce, like Scott's parents did?"

How could you divorce a man when you were going in hiding from him? she'd thought, but she'd hugged her little boy and said that the only thing she was absolutely sure of was that she loved him more than anything in the whole, wide world—and that they were going to move to Atlanta and have fun.

Faith sighed as she slipped into her suit jacket.

They'd moved, at least. The fun part was yet to come, though Peter was content enough. He liked his new friends and the twins' mother, Anne, was great about watching him when Faith needed to go on an interview. Faith reciprocated by watching the twins on the evenings their baby-sitter didn't show up in time for Anne to get to her job as a night cashier at the convenience store up the block.

All in all, things weren't so bad. Faith sighed and ran a comb through her hair. If she only had a job. If she only had some money.

If she only weren't so afraid Cole would find Peter.

He never made threats, he'd said, he only made promises.

And he'd promised to take Peter from her. She didn't doubt that he'd do it, that he was already looking for them. The boy she'd known had grown into a ruthless man who would stop at nothing to get what he wanted.

He'd wanted her and she'd tumbled straight into his trap.

Now he wanted the child he believed was Ted's. Faith shuddered. At least she hadn't told him the truth about Peter. If he'd known her son was really his...

No. She wasn't going to think about that. The possibilities were too frightening.

Faith looked into the mirror one last time, gathered her comb and compact, a lipstick and a couple of tissues and tucked them into her purse. Did she looked like a woman who could sell children's clothing at Macy's?

"Yes," she said to her reflection, "yes, I do."

She smoothed down her skirt and did a last-minute check to make sure she had everything. Keys. The last of her dwindling supply of cash. Okay. She took a deep breath. She was ready.

"Don't worry," Anne had said, when Faith brought Peter to her door earlier in the morning. "He'll be safe." And when Faith looked at her, startled, the other woman had smiled. "You don't have to tell me details but I can tell you've got some kind of problem. Is it with your ex? Does he want to take Peter from you?"

"Something like that," Faith had murmured, because what more could she possibly have said? That her ex was still her husband? That he was a ruthless man who had condemned her as a heartless schemer, and that she was the worst kind of fool because sometimes, in the darkness of the night, she lay awake and wept for the quiet part of her soul that was foolish enough to still love him?

"Stop it," she said firmly, and started toward the door. Something was lying under the table... Ah. She bent down and picked up the small plastic car that was Peter's latest pride and joy.

"Oh, boy," he'd said, when the car had tumbled from the

cereal box this morning, "wait until Jimmy and Joey see this!"

She smiled as she pocketed the toy. Peter would come looking for the car as soon as he realized he'd forgotten it. Well, she could drop it off at Anne's on her way out...

The doorbell rang. Faith's smile broadened. Peter, she thought. He'd already figured out that he'd left his prize behind.

"Sweetheart," she said as she opened the door, "I was just going to bring this to—"

It wasn't her son. It was Cole.

She cried out in shock and tried to push the door closed. He must have expected that because he jammed his shoulder against the it at the same moment and the door flew open, propelling her backward.

Cole stepped into the apartment and shut the door behind him. Faith's heart leaped. This was her worst nightmare come true. He'd found her. He'd found Peter. How could she have been so careless? Opening the door like that, without putting her eye to the peephole? Without at least asking, "Who's there?" Hadn't she warned Peter about those very things? Hadn't she lectured him? Hadn't she set out a whole procedure and just violated it?

"Hello, Faith," Cole said.

She swallowed dryly. "How—how did you find us?"

"You left a trail like an elephant in a crockery shop." He looked around the room, his face expressionless, but she knew what he saw, the cracked plaster, the time-stained walls, the sagging furniture. "Nice place you and the boy have here."

"Get out," she said shakily. "Get out, or I'll call the police."

Cole arched one eyebrow. "Go ahead. Call them. What will you tell them when they get here? That you're not in the mood for a civilized talk with your husband?"

Peter, she thought, *Peter, sweetheart, stay where you are. Don't come back here. Don't come back!*

"What do you want, Cole?"

You, he wanted to say, but he had the feeling she wasn't

ready to hear that yet. She might not ever be ready to hear it. His heart ached as he looked at her. She was wearing the suit she'd worn that day she'd come to Jergen's office but it hung loosely on her now. She'd lost weight, she looked tired, and it was his fault. Everything was his fault. He'd taken the one good thing in his life and destroyed it, not once but twice.

"Well?" Faith dug her hands into her pockets and lifted her chin. "What do you want?"

"Where's Peter?"

"He's not here. And you won't find him. I've—I've sent him away, where he'll be safe."

"Yeah." Cole heaved out a breath. "That's just as well. We need to talk."

"I have nothing to say to you."

He nodded. "I know. But I have things to say to you."

"There's nothing you could tell me that I'd be interested in hearing."

"Faith—"

"No. No, for the first time since you came into my life again, I'm not going to listen to you. You could sing 'Dixie' while standing on your head. You could do Shakespeare while balancing on one foot, and I still wouldn't give a damn!"

"I deserve all that."

"Oh, please. Don't try and be humble. It doesn't become you. And it won't work. I am not going to listen to a thing you—"

"How about if I told you I paid a visit on Jessie?"

Faith's mouth dropped open. She looked at him in disbelief. "Ted's Jessie?"

"I found a letter addressed to—to Jessie in Ted's papers. So I decided…" Cole cleared his throat. Dammit, he'd been walking around with this for almost a week and he still couldn't just come straight out and say it. "Faith? Jessie is—Jessie isn't a woman."

There was anguish in his voice, so much that Faith could feel her anger slipping away. "Yes," she said gently. "I know."

"You know?"

"I've always known. Ted never lied to me."

"My brother—" She could see him searching for the strength to say the words. "My brother was gay."

Faith nodded. "Yes," she said softly.

"He never said anything. I mean, I never knew. I mean…" Cole took a rasping breath. "Why didn't he tell me? Did he think I'd have stopped loving him? Hell, he was my brother!"

"You were his hero," she said softly. "He was afraid he'd disappoint you." She lifted her hand, wanting to touch him, to ease the pain she saw in his hunched shoulders and dark eyes, but too many secrets still separated them, always would separate them, and she let her hand fall to her side. "He tried to be like everyone else, he said. Tried to—to like women but he just… He couldn't. He told me everything, Cole. And he made me promise that I'd never tell you."

"And you kept that promise, even after the terrible things I said about you."

"I gave Ted my word," she said simply. "I loved him. He was—he was the brother I never had, the best friend I'd always wanted. I'd never have done anything to hurt him."

"There were letters," Cole said. "Notes from—from Jessie to Ted. And from Ted to Jessie. I read them. They sounded like love letters…" He gave a choked laugh. "Hell, they *were* love letters. How could I possibly have known they'd been written by…? Faith, I was wrong. I don't expect you to forgive me but—but…" He hesitated. Was it too late? She was listening but she wasn't looking at him the way she once had, as if he were her world just as she was his. "Faith. Baby, I want you to know that I understand about Peter."

Her mouth went dry. "You do?"

"Yes." He took a deep breath. "You were lonely. Ted was—he was fighting against what he knew he was, I guess, trying to prove he could have feelings for women."

Faith shook her head. "It wasn't like that," she whispered.

"No." Cole grasped her shoulders. "No, you don't have to explain. See, it was all my fault. I didn't leave town because I wanted to. I *had* to. Somebody accused me of something and… It's a long story. The bottom line is that I couldn't prove my innocence without dragging you into it.''

"Me?" she said in surprise.

He nodded. "That last night was every dream come true." He reached out, touched the back of his hand to her cheek. "Proving I'd hadn't done anything wrong meant telling my old man and the sheriff that you and I were together that night. And there wasn't a way I'd do that. I loved you too much."

"And now?" she asked softly, her eyes searching his for the truth. "Do you still love me, or was that only a dream, too?"

Cole slipped his arms around her. "I'll always love you. Don't you know that? I'll love you forever, baby, if you'll just give me another chance."

Faith's eyes glittered with tears of happiness. "Oh, Cole. If you only knew how I missed you. All those years, alone, wondering why you'd left me…''

"I'll never leave you again," he said gruffly. He bent his head, brushed his mouth over hers. "And I'll love my brother's son as if he were my own."

Now, she thought, and she lay her hands, palms flat, against his chest. "Cole." She looked up into his eyes. "Peter *is* your own."

At first, she thought he hadn't understood. Then she felt his muscles tense beneath her touch.

"Peter is—is mine?"

"Yes, my darling. He's yours." Faith framed her husband's face with her hands. "Ted came to see me a few weeks after you'd left town. He asked if I was okay, did I need anything, and I—I blurted out that I was pregnant. He was wonderful, Cole. He said I owed our child your name. He asked me to marry him. I said—I said I would never really be his wife and that was when he told me the truth about himself…''

"Mine," Cole said, and let out a whoop. "The kid is mine!" His arms closed around her and he waltzed her around the tiny room. "I have a son."

Faith laughed as they whirled in circles. "I was going to tell you in New York, the morning after we made love, but—"

"But I was an idiot," Cole said gruffly, and kissed her. Faith put her arms around his neck. When the kiss ended, he gathered her close against him. They stood that way for a few minutes, and then she leaned back in his arms.

"Peter doesn't know."

"Pete," Cole said, and grinned. "That's good. This way, we can tell him together."

"He misses you something awful. He hasn't stopped talking about you."

"Yeah." Cole cleared his throat. "Well, I haven't stopped talking about him, either."

Suddenly, the door flew open. "Mom? You know that car I found in the cereal box..." Peter's eyes widened. "Cole?"

"Yeah, champ." Cole squatted down and held out his arms. "Did you miss me?"

Peter ran to his father and threw himself into his arms. "Mom said you had to go away."

"I did. But I'm back. And I'm never going to leave you again." Cole stood up straight and put one arm around his wife. "Never," he said softly.

"Never," Faith said, and she wondered what she'd ever done to deserve such incredible happiness.

It was silly to have another wedding, Faith said. Yeah, Cole said, that was the truth. They were already married. They had a certificate to prove it.

But their son kept reminding them that he should have been there, when his mom and dad said 'I do.' Cole kept looking at his beautiful wife and imagining how she'd have looked as a bride. Faith kept remembering how gorgeous her handsome husband had been in his tux.

And so, on a hot, perfect August afternoon, they invited some of Cole's friends—Faith's friends, too, now—to what they claimed would be a small party.

It was, instead, a wedding.

They were married in the evening, on the flower-bedecked terrace of Cole's penthouse high above the city. Faith was beautiful in a long white gown of pearl-studded lace. She had a pair of antique gold combs in her hair, a gift from her son who'd spent an entire day shopping with his father. Cole was breathtakingly handsome in his black tux.

It was, the guests all agreed, a wonderful wedding.

And, the groom said softly to his wife, as she lay in his arms later that night, it was just the beginning of a long and wonderful life.

Coming Next Month

THE BEST HAS JUST GOTTEN BETTER!

#2229 THE CITY-GIRL BRIDE Penny Jordan
When elegant city girl Maggie Russell is caught in a country flood, rugged Finn Gordon comes to her rescue. He takes her to his farmhouse, laughs at her impractical designer clothes—and then removes them…piece by piece….

#2230 A RICH MAN'S TOUCH Anne Mather
The arrival of businessman Gabriel Webb in Rachel's life is about to change everything! She isn't prepared when he touches emotions in her that she has carefully hidden away. But is Gabriel interested in only a fleeting affair?

#2231 THE PROSPECTIVE WIFE Kim Lawrence
Matt's family are constantly trying to find him a wife, so he is instantly suspicious of blond, beautiful Kat. She's just as horrified to be suspected of being a prospective wife, but soon the talk of bedding and wedding starts to sound dangerously attractive—to both of them….

#2232 HIS MIRACLE BABY Kate Walker
Morgan didn't know why Ellie had left him. It was obvious she'd still been in love with him. But when he found her, to his shock, she had the most adorable baby girl he'd ever seen. Had Ellie found another man or was this baby Morgan's very own miracle?

#2233 SURRENDER TO THE SHEIKH Sharon Kendrick
The last thing Rose expected was to go on assignment to Prince Khalim's kingdom of Maraban. He treated her more like a princess than an employee. Rose knew she could never really be his princess—but their need for each other was so demanding….

#2234 BY MARRIAGE DIVIDED Lindsay Armstrong
Bryn Wallis chose Fleur as his assistant because marriage was definitely not on her agenda—and that suited him perfectly. The last thing he wanted was any romantic involvement. Only, soon he began to find Fleur irresistible….

Three of romance's most talented craftsmen come together in one special collection.

New York Times bestselling authors

Jayne Ann Krentz

Tess Gerritsen

National bestselling author

Stella Cameron

in

Stolen Memories

With plenty of page-turning passion and dramatic storytelling, this volume promises many memorable hours of reading enjoyment!

Coming to your favorite retail outlet in February 2002.

HARLEQUIN®
Makes any time special ®

We're delighted to announce that

A Mediterranean Marriage

is taking place in

HARLEQUIN®
Presents

This month, in THE BELLINI BRIDE by Michelle Reid, #2224

Marco Bellini has to choose a suitable wife.
Will he make an honest woman of his
beautiful mistress, Antonia?

In March you are invited to the wedding of
Rio Lombardi and Holly Samson
in THE ITALIAN'S WIFE by Lynne Graham, #2235

When Holly, a homeless young woman, collapses in front of
Rio Lombardi's limousine, he feels compelled to take her and
her baby son home with him. Holly can't believe it when Rio
lavishes her with food, clothes…and a wedding ring….

Harlequin Presents®
The world's bestselling romance series.
Seduction and passion guaranteed!

Available wherever Harlequin books are sold.

HARLEQUIN®
Makes any time special ®
Visit us at www.eHarlequin.com

HPJANMM